"Dad!" Luke tugged furiously on Joe's jeans. "It's her!"

"Who?" Joe was still staring at her and thinking that he hadn't been so blown away by the sight of a woman in years. She had dainty feet, encased in fancy sandals in a sparkling silver color. Smooth, trim calves. Cute knees. A long, bulky white jacket—he could have done without that. Delicate hands—no rings, he noted. Pale, peach-colored lips, eyes as blue as the sky. An absolutely dazzling smile, directed at his son.

"The tooth fairy!" Luke said.

"Luke, there's no such thing as—"

"Uh-ummm." The woman cleared her throat loudly. She gave him a conspiratorial wink.

Being this close to a woman, having her smile at him baffled Joe. How could he consider allowing another woman into his life? One had been more than enough.

But when he looked at this woman, he felt uneasy. Here, he thought, was a woman who just might be able to change his mind....

Dear Reader,

When Patricia Kay was a child, she could be found hiding somewhere...reading. "Ever since I was old enough to realize someone wrote books and they didn't just magically appear, I dreamed of writing," she says. And this month Special Edition is proud to publish Patricia's twenty-second novel, *The Millionaire and the Mom*, the next of the STOCKWELLS OF TEXAS series. She admits it isn't always easy keeping her ideas and her writing fresh. What helps, she says, is "nonwriting" activities, such as singing in her church choir, swimming, taking long walks, going to the movies and traveling. "Staying well-rounded keeps me excited about writing," she says.

We have plenty of other fresh stories to offer this month. After finding herself in the midst of an armed robbery with a gun to her back in Christie Ridgway's *From This Day Forward*, Annie Smith vows to chase her dreams.... In the next of A RANCHING FAMILY series by Victoria Pade, Kate McDermot returns from Vegas unexpectedly married and with a *Cowboy's Baby* in her belly! And Sally Tyler Hayes's *Magic in a Jelly Jar* is what young Luke Morgan hopes for by saving his teeth in a jelly jar...because he thinks that his dentist is the tooth fairy and can grant him one wish: a mother! Also, don't miss the surprising twists in *Her Mysterious Houseguest* by Jane Toombs, and an exciting forbidden love story with Barbara Benedict's *Solution: Marriage*.

At Special Edition, fresh, innovative books are our passion. We hope you enjoy them all.

Best,

Karen Taylor Richman
Senior Editor

Please address questions and book requests to:
Silhouette Reader Service
U.S.: 3010 Walden Ave., P.O. Box 1325, Buffalo, NY 14269
Canadian: P.O. Box 609, Fort Erie, Ont. L2A 5X3

Magic in a Jelly Jar

SALLY TYLER HAYES

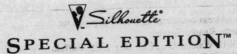

SPECIAL EDITION™

Published by Silhouette Books

America's Publisher of Contemporary Romance

To my son, John, a mathematically gifted and mercenary child who, when he started losing his baby teeth, began with great excitement to count and even do a bit of multiplication in order to figure out what his entire mouth was worth empty of teeth.

And to his first-grade class at St. Mary's, where the loss of each tooth was dutifully charted and graphed as part of their lessons in math.

 SILHOUETTE BOOKS

ISBN 0-373-24390-1

MAGIC IN A JELLY JAR

Visit Silhouette at www.eHarlequin.com

Printed in U.S.A.

Books by Sally Tyler Hayes

Silhouette Special Edition

Magic in a Jelly Jar #1390

Silhouette Intimate Moments

Whose Child Is This? #439
Dixon's Bluff #485
Days Gone By #549
Not His Wife #611
Our Child? #671
Homecoming #700
Temporary Family #738
Second Father #753
Wife, Mother...Lover? #818
*Dangerous To Love #903
*Spies, Lies and Lovers #940
*Cinderella and the Spy #1001
*Her Secret Guardian #1012

*Division One

SALLY TYLER HAYES

lives in South Carolina with her husband, son and daughter. A former journalist for a South Carolina newspaper, she fondly remembers that her decision to write and explore the frontiers of romance came at about the same time she discovered, in junior high, that she'd never be able to join the crew of the *Starship Enterprise*.

Happy and proud to be a stay-home mom, she is thrilled to be living her lifelong dream of writing romances.

Dear Tooth Fairy,

My name is Luke, and I saw you last week. You came to my school to talk about teeth, and you were so pretty. I gotta big problem, and I know you're the one who can help me. I tried everythin' else and nothin' worked. Santa didn't help, even though I was real good. I wished on my birthday candles, but that didn't work. I wished on the first star at night, but that didn't work. But you can make everything all right. I saw you, and I know you can do real magic. I gotta plan, too. I'm gonna collect a hundred baby teeth, no matter what it takes! I figure that'll be enough. And I'll give 'em to you and make my wish, and you can bring my mother back....

Love,

Luke

Prologue

"Aw, c'mon, Jenny. It won't hurt. Promise."

The girl knew he was lying. After all, he was a boy, and at seven, Jenny knew all about boys. He'd say anything to get what he wanted. And once he did, he'd be off to charm some other girl. Jenny's mother had told her older sister all about boys one night when she didn't know Jenny was listening.

"Please. I neeeed it," he whined pitifully.

She'd heard about that before, too. "I told you—no."

"Give you a quarter."

"I heard you offered Betsy fifty cents!"

"'Kay. Fifty cents."

That made her stop and think. Fifty cents would buy her a soda after school. Or a candy bar. Curiosity made her ask, "But what d'you want with a dumb old tooth, anyway?"

"Shh," Luke said. "It's a secret."

Jenny tried her perfect-princess smile on him. "You can tell me. I'm your best friend."

"But you're a *girl*," he said, as if it was the ultimate insult.

"I'm still your friend." Her bottom lip started to tremble.

"'Kay, you're my friend. Now, do we have a deal?"

"Quarters first," she insisted, because she'd done business with boys before.

Luke fished them out of his pocket and handed them over.

"Promise it won't hurt?"

"'Course not. Mine didn't hurt a bit." He showed her a gap-toothed grin. "B'sides, it's already loose, right?"

Jenny nodded, just starting to get scared. She'd never lost a tooth before, and she knew she was being a sucker to give this one to Luke for fifty cents. After all, the tooth fairy would probably give her at least two dollars. Some of the kids in the class who'd already lost a tooth had gotten three dollars.

But Luke was up to something, and he always had the best ideas. He must want this tooth for something really important, especially to give up fifty cents.

"Open up," Luke said, coming toward her with one of the laces from his shoe dangling from his hand.

Next thing she knew, Luke had nearly his whole hand in her mouth trying to tie that lace around her tooth. Jenny tried to yell, but that didn't work. She was gagging, instead. She tried to tell Luke she'd changed her mind, but he kept struggling with the shoelace and her loose tooth.

Finally she got so mad she bit him.

Luke screamed and jerked his hand out of her mouth.

Jenny looked down and saw her tooth stuck in the side of Luke's thumb, and then she screamed, too.

Chapter One

"He what?"

Leaning against the open door of his pickup, his cell phone cradled against his ear and noise from the construction site making it nearly impossible to hear, Joe Morgan was sure there had to be some mistake. Even though Luke was only in first grade, Joe had already gotten some strange phone calls from school. This, however, was the strangest.

"What was he doing with his hand in a girl's mouth?"

"Trying to pull the tooth, I believe," said Miss Reynolds, Luke's twenty-something, ever-so-proper, first-grade teacher. "Maybe Luke will explain that to you. He certainly wouldn't say anything more to me."

Joe could just imagine the story Luke would tell about this particular antic. Luke was always up to something, always scheming and planning, always into some sort of trouble.

"He broke the girl's tooth?"

"Apparently the tooth was already loose. When he tried to get it out of Jenny's mouth, it hurt. So she bit him. When he pulled his hand out of her mouth, the tooth came with it. It was stuck in the side of his thumb."

"Wonderful." Joe could just imagine what this girl's parents must think of him and his son.

"Neither one of them is hurt. Not really. They both just want the tooth. Luke claims he bought it from Jenny for fifty cents."

"While it was still in her mouth?" Joe frowned. Other kids were content to play doctor. His son had to be original.

"Honestly, Mr. Morgan, that's all I've managed to get out of them. The children know they're in trouble and are refusing to talk. We also can't find the tooth, something that's causing them considerable anxiety."

Joe sighed.

Ever since Luke had lost his first tooth—no, even before that—he'd been fascinated with the whole idea of losing teeth. He was definitely up to something. Joe had no idea what. Raising two little kids on his own, now that his wife was gone, was proving to be almost more than he could handle. But he never thought he'd get tripped up so thoroughly over something like teeth.

"I'm afraid you're going to have to come in again, Mr. Morgan. We need to talk about what's going on with Luke."

Joe groaned, but he was at the school at three-twenty, right on schedule. He parked his pickup amidst enough minivans and SUVs to stock a car lot, then dusted off his jeans as best he could, sending sawdust flying. His shirt was coated with dust, as well, his cowboy boots caked with dried mud, but there was nothing he could do about that. He worked hard for a living, and by this time of day, it showed.

The school Luke attended was old and steeped in tradition. For more than one hundred years, St. Mark's Academy had educated the well-to-do children of the well-to-do St. Mark's parish, and the family of Joe's former wife had been founding members of the church and the school. His mother-in-law had put the kids' names on the preenrollment list the day they were born, and she'd probably pulled some strings to get them admitted.

Joe felt as if he'd had no choice but to send Luke and Dani there, even if tuition was killing him and he never quite felt at ease inside this building or with the parents of the other students.

Keeping his eyes down, a tight smile on his face, he made his way across the broad sidewalk, where children were waiting to be picked up from school. In their school plaids and white shirts, the girls were neat and tidy, their hair done in sleek ponytails or intricate braids that Joe would never master. The boys, in dark slacks, white shirts and outrageously expensive sneakers, were louder and rougher as they huddled together laughing and talking about their day. His son was probably in Sister Mary Margaret's office. Sister was the principal, and Joe had never met a woman so good at invoking guilt and remorse in his weary soul.

He went to Luke's classroom, with its four neat rows of tiny desks and chairs, every inch of the walls covered with kids' drawings and posters and signs.

Order reigned here, where chaos was king at his home. No wonder Luke didn't fit in, Joe thought.

"Mr. Morgan?"

Luke's teacher, who might have been twenty-five years old, was waiting for him. He felt ancient beside her, though he was only thirty-one. Miss Reynolds, as he'd always called her, because that was what Luke called her and Joe didn't even know her first name, wore a long flowery dress with lace at the collar and the sleeves. Her hair was smoothed back into a neat knot at the back of her head. She always gave him a smile that made him feel like a bowl of cream that had been placed in front of a happy hungry cat. She was husband-hunting, just as he'd feared the first time he came in for one of these little conferences. But Joe wasn't interested in being anyone's husband again.

Luke, he thought, *you're going to pay for this.*

"Ma'am," he said, trying to hide all that he was feeling. If he hadn't left Texas nearly a decade ago, he would have tipped his hat, in that respectful way he'd been taught to greet a lady. Instead, he settled for nodding his head and lowering his eyes.

"Mr. Morgan." She pointed to one of the kiddie chairs. "Please sit."

Joe sank into it and tried not to grimace as his knees rose in front of him. He just loved these chairs.

"I sent Luke to the after-school program so we can have our little talk in private," she said. "Mr. Morgan, I don't mean to pry, but I was wondering if there was anything going on at home that I should know about."

Joe groaned. The teacher smiled sweetly, as if she hadn't asked him to bare his soul to her.

"Sometimes parents aren't aware of it," she said, "but problems at home almost always show up in a child's behavior at school. And if there is a problem, it's best to tell us so we can be prepared and try to offer some extra help and understanding.''

Everyone at his house could use some extra help and understanding, Joe thought. But still, he hated what it would take to get it for them.

''I know that you and Luke's mother are divorced,'' she began, ''and that you have full custody.''

''That's right,'' he said. He'd given the school the bare bones of it on the forms he'd filled out. Who was the custodial parent? Who was authorized to pick up the child from school and who wasn't? Were there any custody issues the school should be aware of? He'd hated that form.

''And the two of you have been separated for…?''

''Thirteen months.'' He could tell her the day, even the hour, if she thought that was necessary.

''And when Luke does see his mother—''

''He doesn't,'' Joe cut in.

''Oh.'' Miss Reynolds looked taken aback. ''Not ever?''

''No.'' Joe's face burned.

''Well…I wish we had known sooner.''

''Sorry,'' he said tightly. It was the first time his wife ever walked out, and he wasn't up on all the proper procedures to follow.

''Look, I don't mean to pry. I was just worried about Luke and trying to understand what was going on. I noticed when we returned after Christmas break a few weeks ago that Luke seemed particularly upset. I thought perhaps something happened at Christmas.''

Joe suspected that Luke asked Santa to bring his mother home for Christmas, and Santa hadn't. Not that

Joe was going to share that particular tidbit with Miss Reynolds.

"Luke is rather quick-tempered lately," she tried. "And irritable."

She could have easily been describing Joe, but again, he didn't say anything about that. Still, she looked like she expected a response.

"It's been a difficult adjustment," he said, which had to be the understatement of the year.

"Well…I'll try to be understanding with Luke in class. And if anything happens, anything you think I should know, please feel free to call me. I'll do anything I can to help Luke."

She smiled and let her hand rest on his knee for a moment. When did women get so forward? Joe wondered. He and Elena had been together for eight years, and he didn't remember women coming on to men this way before. Maybe there was just something about a man alone trying to raise two little kids that brought out that protective streak in some women. They just didn't understand. The last thing Joe wanted was to give another woman a chance to trample all over his heart and his kids' hearts. He rose to go, the movement freeing him from her touch.

"One more thing," Miss Reynolds said, getting to her feet, as well. "Luke seems…obsessed—that's the best word I can think of to describe it—with teeth. All kids this age are excited by the idea, but Luke…"

"I know. I'm not sure why. He won't tell me."

"You're going to have to talk to him," Miss Reynolds said. "We really can't have him trying to pull the other children's teeth here at school."

"Of course." Joe gritted his teeth and promised to have the talk.

"I did have an idea about that. We have a wonderful new children's dentist in town. She came and spoke to the class about taking proper care of their teeth when we did our unit on dental hygiene, and the kids just loved it. Luke was especially attentive that day. He was quite taken with her costume."

"Costume?"

"Yes. She dressed up as the tooth fairy. The kids talked about her visit for weeks."

"A grown woman actually dressed up as the tooth fairy to come talk to schoolkids?"

"Yes. We had a terrific time that day. They're convinced she *is* the tooth fairy."

"Luke talked about her at home, too. I thought he was making it up." Joe hadn't seen his son so animated since his mother had walked out on them.

"I thought you might take him to see her. Maybe she could explain what's proper and what's not when it comes to teeth, and Luke would listen to her."

Miss Reynolds held out a slip of paper. Joe took it and fled from the classroom, clutching the tooth fairy's phone number in his hand.

He wasn't going to call her. He was convinced he could handle this himself without the aid of a woman who dressed up like a fairy. But the next day he got another call from school. Something about an incident in the cafeteria, Luke's hand in someone else's mouth, and a flashlight and more kids who weren't talking. Joe was at a loss. A grown woman in a fairy costume didn't sound so bad anymore.

He got Luke from school and tried not to think about what it would be like to tell his strange tale to the lady dentist. He just hoped she could help.

* * *

When Joe pushed open the front door of the dentist's office, music flowed out. It was some silly jingle that Dani loved, one the purple dinosaur sang.

"Is this place for babies?" Luke asked, insulted to the core.

"No, it's for big kids, too," Joe replied, smiling at the notion that at seven, Luke was big. To Luke, a person was either big or little. There was no in between. Dani, at four, was little. Luke was convinced he was big.

A few moments later the receptionist led them down a hallway colored with a rainbow, one shade dropping out as it made its way into each brightly colored treatment room. Luke drew the blue room, which featured a blue ceiling complete with stars. Luke and Joe stared up at those thousands of glittering stars. Was it a trick of the light or were they truly glittering?

Special paint, he decided. Manufacturers were doing amazing things with paint these days. He'd have to inquire about exactly what brand it was. Some of his clients might be interested.

"Dad!" Luke was tugging on his pant legs. "Look! It glitters! Isn't it cool? And it's a sign. I know it is. This place is magic!"

Joe scoffed. Magic was for seven-year-olds.

Then, just as he turned away, he caught a rush of movement out of the corner of his eye. Turning back, he felt the hair on the back of his neck stand on end. It was crazy, but he could have sworn he'd just seen a star streak across the ceiling. A shooting star.

Joe blinked to clear his vision. It was the middle of the afternoon, he reminded himself, and he was inside staring at a ceiling painted blue and sprayed with fake stars. Nothing moved in the would-be sky, but the stars still glittered. He almost reached up to touch them, to see if it truly was glitter and would rub off on his fingertips.

He was still trying to figure it out when he heard footsteps behind him, then a rich full voice that said, "Hello, you must be Luke."

Joe's son seemed struck dumb, and a moment later Joe supposed they must look like a real pair.

This had to be the fairy.

He took his time looking her over from the bottom up. She had dainty feet, encased in fancy sandals with tiny straps in a sparkling silver color. Smooth trim calves—very nice. Cute little knees, too, peeking out from under a pale skirt that stopped an obliging two inches above her knees. A long loose jacket covered almost all of the rest of her; he could have done without that.

All he could see outside of the jacket was a pair of delicate hands—no rings, he noted—and the enticing curve of her throat and neck. She had pale peach-colored lips, eyes as blue as that fake sky. Her hair was honey-colored and pulled back from her face into an intricate braid Dani would have loved and seriously envied, and it hung to a point halfway down her back. She had dainty moon-shaped earrings, and an absolutely dazzling smile that was directed, full force, at his son, who was positively glowing.

Joe told himself he was being rude, staring at her this way. He simply couldn't help it.

"Dad!" Luke was tugging furiously on Joe's jeans. Bending down, Joe let Luke whisper in his ear, "It's her!"

"Who?" Joe was still staring at her and thinking

that he hadn't been so blown away by the sight of a woman in years. He thought he was over that—that having his and his children's hearts ripped out by a woman who had pledged to love them forever would have cured him.

"The tooth fairy!" Luke whispered loudly enough for the mischievous-looking woman to hear. He looked as if he was ready to explode with excitement. "She came to my school, 'cept she was all dressed up then in the blue dress with the stars. She even had her magic wand with her. I know it's her. And she's real. She's the tooth fairy."

"Luke, there's no such thing as—"

"Uh-hmm." The woman cleared her throat loudly. Joe stopped just in time. "Sorry."

She gave him a conspiratorial wink, then turned to Luke and stuck out her hand. "I'm Dr. Carter. And you are Luke, aren't you? Please tell me I'm in the right room."

Luke took the hand she offered and whispered, "You're her, aren't you?"

"Who?" she said with a smile.

"The tooth fairy." Luke was still whispering, as if he couldn't say it out loud.

She laughed, a sound that invited everyone around to laugh with her. Joe would have, if he'd been able to make a sound.

"But tooth fairies are magic," she said quite seriously. "I'm just a dentist."

Then she pulled a quarter from behind Luke's right ear and handed it to him.

"Wow! Did you see that, Dad? She *is* magic."

Dr. Carter was still grinning down at his son. Her hand headed for Luke's other ear, and before Joe could say anything, she pulled a plastic spider ring from behind Luke's ear.

"Wow!" Luke just stared up at her and grinned.

"So, what seems to be the problem here, Luke? Or are you just here for a checkup?"

"I dunno," Luke said, Mr. Innocent now.

"I need to talk to you," Joe said, not wanting to explain the problem in front of Luke.

"All right." Dr. Carter turned back to his son. "Luke, I have a very special chair that goes up and down when you press this little button. How 'bout I let you sit in it and take it up and down?"

"Can I really?"

"Sure." She helped Luke into the chair and showed him the button. "But you have to promise that when Mary comes in to count your teeth and when I check them, you'll leave the chair alone. Deal?"

She held out her palm. Luke slapped it with enthusiasm. "Deal!"

The chair was revving up and down when the dentist led Joe from the room.

"Don't the kids wear out the chairs?" he said.

"Eventually, but it makes them happy to take them up and down." She said it as if that was the only thing that mattered—making the children happy. "Besides, it's impossible to keep them from playing with the chairs, kind of like telling them to be still or to stay out of the mud on a rainy day. So I cut a deal with them—they can play for a minute, get it out of their system, then they have to leave the chairs alone while we work."

She led him down the hall and to the right. Joe found himself watching the muscles flex in those trim calves of hers as she walked, and he wished she'd take off that white coat so he could see what was beneath it. She opened a heavy wooden door to the right, then offered him a seat in front of her desk. The desk was old and solid, made of polished cherry, and he guessed it weighed a ton. Joe couldn't help but admire it.

"They don't make pieces like this these days," he said, running a finger around the intricate trim work.

"I know. This was my father's. In fact, almost all the furniture in here was his." She stood beside a big leather swivel chair that seemed as if it would swallow her.

Joe glanced around the room, saw bookshelves overflowing with thick heavy texts, a dozen or so plants of all sizes and shapes that almost took over the room, and another glass cabinet with dozens of fairy figurines inside it.

"You're really into this tooth-fairy thing, aren't you?"

"My father was. He was a dentist, too, and he's been collecting fairies since before I was born. He died last year."

"Sorry," Joe said. "I didn't mean to bring up bad memories."

She shrugged as if it didn't matter. But Joe knew it did. The woman who'd been so animated in the other room with his son was quite different now. No mischievous smile waited on her lips, no twinkle in those amazing blue eyes. Joe wished he hadn't taken her smile away.

"So." She moved to the front of the desk, then leaned against it. "What's wrong with Luke?"

Joe ran through the list in his head. Luke wouldn't give up his teeth. In fact, the ones he *had* given up to the tooth fairy, he'd cried and begged to buy back within days of giving them up. He played dentist at school, tearing out Jenny's tooth, and was in some kid's mouth with a flashlight in the lunchroom earlier that day. He had a mother who'd left and probably wasn't ever coming back. How much of that could Joe share with this woman who pulled quarters from behind little boys' ears to make them smile?

"It can't be that bad," she offered, then reached a hand out to him.

Joe sat back in the chair. He felt her fingertips brush his chest above the pocket of the clean shirt he'd donned in the truck before he picked Luke up from school, and then she pulled a long yellow scarf from his shirt pocket. It seemed to take forever, and Joe was baffled by the whole procedure.

Being this close to the woman, having her touch him in such an inconsequential way, having her smile at him, then blush as if she'd embarrassed herself—it all baffled him.

Because it felt so good.

Time to go out on a date, he supposed, dismissing the idea just as quickly as he considered allowing another woman into his life. One had been more than enough.

And then he looked up at the woman with the yellow scarf in her small elegant hands, a flush of color in her cheeks.

Here, he thought with flashes of unease shooting through him, was a woman who just might be able to change his mind about that. Not that he wanted it to change. He certainly didn't intend to let another woman get anywhere near his kids.

Samantha froze, like a mischievous kid caught red-handed, as Joe Morgan stood there, staring at her. He didn't so much as blink, didn't say anything. He looked bewildered at first, then impossibly stern.

"I…I'm so sorry," she stammered, as heat flooded her cheeks. She explained as best she could. "Force of habit."

"Habit?" the striking dark-haired man said.

She nodded and tried not to stumble over her words. "I do little tricks. To make the children smile. And…"

It had been sheer impulse. She'd seen him sitting there looking sad, so she'd done the first thing that popped into her head—pull a silk scarf from his shirt pocket. Except he was no scared little boy. He was a man. A very attractive man. And she'd just made a fool of herself.

"You looked…troubled," she said, wondering if he'd felt anything at all when she touched him. *She* certainly had. Something like a little jolt of static electricity, only better. Something like magic, except Samantha wasn't sure she believed in magic anymore. She suddenly felt foolish for all the years she had believed. It seemed so naive now.

"It's been a difficult day," he said.

"I'm sorry," she said, thinking she'd like to know about his day, like to know if his had truly been nearly as bad as hers and whether he had any idea how to fix it. Maybe he could tell her how to fix hers, how to fix everything. He looked like a man who fixed things.

Samantha stared at him, at long legs encased in well-worn jeans, snug in all the right places, cowboy boots splattered with dried mud, but a clean shirt, the sleeves rolled up nearly to his elbows. He had the kind of all-over tan worn by a man who worked outside year-round, and the lean corded muscles in his arms indicated he did something physical and likely did it well.

He dusted off his jeans—maybe because he'd caught her staring—and sawdust went flying.

"Sorry. I came straight from work," he said. "I'm a mess by this time of day."

"No problem," she assured him, fingering the shapeless white coat she wore. "I get messy, too. Which is why I live in these."

She thought about taking off the ugly white coat, but decided that might be too obvious, and she'd never been obvious with a man.

"You must work outside," she guessed. To her, that was a bold move.

"Yes. I'm a builder."

He said it as if she might find something objectionable in that. She didn't. He was obviously a strong man who was good with his hands, and he was gorgeous, in a rough-and-tumble sort of way. What was there for any woman to object to?

Samantha's only problem was that she'd lost all track of the conversation and forgotten the reason he was here. *His son.* That was it. Did that mean he had a wife, too?

She checked as discreetly as possible and saw no ring on his left hand. Women did that these days, she'd found. Regularly. For some women it was an automatic action. Check the hand. No ring? No telltale pale band of skin on the ring finger? He wasn't shy about giving out his home phone number? Didn't find excuses why you shouldn't call him at home? He was likely single.

Samantha hadn't put any of those tactics into practice—until now—but she'd learned all the signs that indicated a married man. Just in case she was ever interested enough to check out a man.

So far, she hadn't been. She'd hardly met any men at all since she'd been here. At the dentist's office it was almost all mothers and children, which made this man even more intriguing.

Oh, jeez, Samantha admitted, he'd be intriguing under any circumstances, and she was staring quite rudely, probably making a fool of herself. Not that she'd ever take this any farther than a mild flirtation—just for practice. She was sadly out of practice, after all. It showed in everything she'd said and done to him. She could relate to seven-year-olds better than grown men. And he had a seven-year-old. An adorable one, which made him strictly off-limits, him and his kid.

"Mr. Morgan—"

"Joe," he cut in.

"Joe." She liked the sound of his name on her lips. "About Luke—what can I do for him? And for you?"

Looking wary again, Joe just stared at her, then finally started to talk. "Luke has been behaving strangely lately."

"You can tell me," she encouraged because this seemed to be so difficult for him.

"It's...I don't understand it. He's obsessed with teeth. Yesterday, on the playground at school, he tried to pull out a little girl's tooth. Today in the cafeteria, he had a flashlight and his hand inside a little boy's mouth..."

"Oh." Samantha considered for a minute. "Does he by any chance go to St. Mark's?"

"Yes. Why?"

She'd definitely embarrassed him now, and she felt bad.

"I've been getting some calls from St. Mark's. I think I saw his patient, Jenny, yesterday. I've been wondering about my competitor, actually."

"The little girl's all right, isn't she? Please tell me Luke didn't do any damage."

Samantha wanted to reassure him, felt an almost overwhelming urge to touch him. With the kids, she was generous with her smiles, her laughter, the touch of her hand on a shoulder or a big hug. But this was a man, she reminded herself again. And she'd already made a fool of herself with her little bag of tricks.

"Jenny's fine." She managed to keep her hands to herself and rushed on, "She would have lost the tooth in a few days, anyway."

"Thank goodness for that," he said.

"So, what else is Luke doing?"

"He's so caught up in this whole tooth thing. At first I thought it was money. Luke loves money. But after he lost his first tooth and put it under his pillow, the…uh…"

"The tooth fairy came to visit?" she suggested.

"Yes, and he got his money. Then he decided he'd rather have the tooth back. He came and asked if he could buy it back."

Samantha laughed. "I hope you agreed."

"Yes. He put his two dollars under his pillow without complaining at all about the loss of the money, and the next morning, there was his tooth."

"Good," Samantha said. He was willing to play along, for the sake of his son. "So what did he do with the tooth?"

"He put it in a jelly jar on the shelf in the top of

his closet, along with the other three teeth he's lost. He's saving them.''

''For what?''

Joe shrugged. ''I don't know. He hasn't said. Do you think you could explain to my son that dentists are the only people allowed to pull teeth?''

''Of course.''

''He's up to something. I don't know what.''

''Something to do with baby teeth? And magic? And wishes?''

Joe nodded.

Once again she wanted to touch him, to soothe him just a bit, maybe make him smile again. She had a feeling he wasn't normally such a stern-looking man.

''What does Luke want?''

Joe swore so softly she could barely hear it, then added quietly, ''I'm afraid to ask.''

''Something that's not within your power to give?'' she guessed.

Joe nodded again.

Samantha couldn't help but wonder where Mrs. Morgan was right now, and she sensed that was the answer to Luke's wishes and to his father's obvious discomfort. She wouldn't pry any further, because she suspected this man's pride had taken a beating somewhere along the way. But taking a closer look at his left hand, she now found that strip of paler skin that told her, until recently, he'd worn what she suspected was a wedding ring.

Poor Luke, she thought. What happened to his mother?

''I'll give Luke my standard speech on the importance of taking care of teeth, letting them come out when they're ready—all that good stuff,'' she said.

And she'd throw in a few more magic tricks to make Luke smile.

"Thank you. I appreciate it."

And then, because there was nothing left to do, she excused herself to go talk to Luke and left Joe in the peace and quiet of her office.

She was back fifteen minutes later, having left Luke in the waiting room admiring one of her displays of fairy figurines and not sure she'd been any help at all. Joe Morgan stood with his back to her, his impossibly broad shoulders seeped in tension. She wished there was something she could do to soothe him, too.

"Hi," she said, walking in and closing the door behind her.

He turned around and looked at her, waiting, obviously hoping. She hated disappointing him.

"I'm sorry. Luke has a mouthful of beautiful absolutely healthy teeth and a whole lot of secrets. I tried my best, but I couldn't get him to crack."

Joe smiled. "Really put on the pressure, did you, Doc?"

"I tried," she reassured him. "He's very bright. He asked me all sorts of questions about baby teeth. How many kids have and when they start to lose them, how long it takes before they're all gone. He says he has a friend who's good with numbers who's going to help him figure everything out. He mentioned something about a formula. I hope we're talking mathematical and not chemical."

Joe laughed. "I'll lock up his chemistry set."

"That would probably be a good idea."

"Luke is a schemer. Always has been. He gets an

idea in his head, and he doesn't let go of it. Not for anything.''

"Which is not necessarily a bad trait.''

"In an adult. It's hell in a kid, especially when you're the one trying to raise him.''

Samantha shrugged, telling herself not to get drawn in too deeply. She was just here to take care of kids' teeth. She always got in too deep, always cared too much. Surely she'd learned her lesson by now.

"I'm sure you'll figure out what he's up to. Or he'll tell you,'' she said. "I showed Luke all my instruments and explained to him all the things I use to pull out a tooth safely, and I thought that would do it. But I didn't like the gleam in his eye. I was afraid he'd be off stealing a pair of pliers or an adjustable wrench from your toolbox and using what I told him to be even more efficient at dentistry than he already is. I hope that wasn't a mistake.''

"I'll lock up my tools, too," Joe said. "Just in case.''

"Good. My next idea was to tell him he could be a dentist, but he had to suffer through a ton of schooling and pass all sorts of tests first to be licensed. That may have made some headway with him—the idea that he could be in trouble for practicing dentistry without a license.''

Joe laughed out loud then. She saw little crinkles at the corners of his dark eyes and his mouth. His shoulders shook and he relaxed, at least for a second. How about that? she mused. She'd made him laugh, really laugh. She felt as good as she did when one of her little tricks won her a genuine smile from a kid.

"You're very good, Doc. I'm impressed.''

She blushed at the praise, thinking she'd thoroughly enjoyed her time with the Morgan men.

"He seemed to like me. Quite a bit," she admitted. "So my third and final strategy was to tell Luke that if he insisted on taking care of all his classmates' teeth, pretty soon I wouldn't have anything to do, that he'd ruin my job."

"That's perfect," Joe said. "I appreciate it. More than I can say."

"He's a delightful little boy."

"Yeah, he is."

"Take good care of him. And call me if there's anything else I can do," she offered, wondering if he'd take her up on that, if she'd ever see either one of them again.

Joe Morgan took her hand in both of his. Her entire arm started to tingle in an unsettling way. They stood there, staring at each other. She felt a strange sense of connection with him, something she didn't want to lose. Which was crazy. She didn't even know him. She didn't know anything about him, except that he was too handsome for her own good, she felt a little charge of electricity when he touched her, and he had a great little boy.

Samantha pulled away, because that was how it had to be. She had to look out for herself this time. She had to be smart, safe.

"Thanks, Doc," he said softly.

"You're welcome," she said, fighting this odd urge to beg him to stay.

He turned and walked to the door, was almost gone when she thought of something.

"Joe?"

He turned to face her again. "Yes?"

''I may have convinced Luke to stop practicing dentistry, but he's absolutely convinced I have magical powers. I'm afraid my little tricks with the coins and things just made it worse. He thinks I'm the tooth fairy.''

Joe considered, then replied, ''I'll take care of it.''

Samantha nodded, wondering what he'd say. That there was no such thing as magic? No wishes coming true? No miracles left in this world?

She hoped not, even though she supposed it was true. But Samantha had seen children who'd stopped believing in magic, who'd been robbed of their illusions, and she didn't want Luke to be one of them.

Chapter Two

It was much later that evening when Samantha shed her white coat, which she wore to guard her clothes but also for the deep pockets where she stored the tricks of her trade. She took out the glow-in-the-dark toothbrushes, the magic disappearing coins, the fat tongue depressor that turned into a bouquet of flowers and the magic set of teeth that chattered around on tabletops when she wound them up.

Her last patient was long gone, as well as the office staff. There was nothing left to do but go back to the house she'd rented temporarily while she tried out this town, this practice. While she decided whether it was any easier to be here, far away from everyone she'd left behind, everyone she'd lost.

She felt absolutely alone that night, absolutely lost.

She had put the length of the country between her and everyone she knew, everything that was familiar, thinking to start over in a brand-new place. Brand-new house, if she ever got around to finding one. Brand-new practice, if she made up her mind and exercised her option to buy this one. Brand-new what else? she wondered.

Man, came the answer, the image of a certain one coming into her head.

Brand-new kid? She knew better. She did.

So she swiveled around in her chair to face the window of the office that she'd occupied for all of six weeks now and that was starting to feel familiar, thanks to all of the things she'd brought. Her gaze eventually landed on the small glass cabinet in the corner. It had small framed drawings, porcelain figurines, carvings, even a sculpture her father had made, all of his favorite image, the tooth fairy. They always made her smile, always made her patients smile.

It was mostly her father's collection, one of his most prized possessions. He'd willed them to her, and now she displayed some of them in her office. It added an air of magic to the place, which her father had taught her to use to help get past the fear some children had of dentists.

Little children should never be afraid, her father always said.

She closed her eyes and thought, *But I'm afraid, Daddy. I'm so afraid.*

Afraid that she would always feel this bad, this sad and alone, this lost, and here were no little magic tricks to make it better. No fairy dust raining down on her.

Which made her think of Luke and Joe. They seemed afraid, too. Sad and lost and hurting. Maybe that was why she found herself so drawn to them, why she felt so bereft without them.

She'd been happy today, just for a little bit. Happy with Luke and Joe. She'd felt what seemed to be a little spark of pure magic, and it had frightened her.

So she had to remember all that she'd lost and the reason she had to stay away from them. It shouldn't be that hard to remember, especially not here. There was a spot at the end of the credenza, just to the right by the droopy-looking potted fern she'd lugged all the way from Seattle, a spot where she'd always kept a favorite photograph of the girls.

Maybe it had been a mistake to leave the photos behind. She'd debated that point with herself for what seemed like hours, and in the end, she'd left the photos, along with a big chunk of her heart.

Samantha knew she had to safeguard that battered heart of hers now. She had to be careful and cautious and use her head.

No men, she told herself even more sternly. Especially men with kids. If she'd learned anything else in the past four years, surely she'd learned that. No men and, please, God, no more falling in love with kids who didn't belong to her.

Dr. Carter let Luke keep the quarter and the spider ring. Best of all, she gave him a glow-in-the-dark toothbrush. When Joe brought him home, Luke hid in the closet with the toothbrush all evening watching it glow. He swore the toothbrush was magic, that Dr. Carter was magic and that she was really the tooth fairy in disguise.

Dani wailed off and on all night after they picked her up from late-stay at school. Because she didn't get to see the tooth fairy, because she still hadn't lost a tooth and because she hadn't gotten a quarter, a spider ring or a glow-in-the-dark toothbrush.

Once he'd finally gotten them into bed, Joe put a hand to the back of his neck and tried to work out the tension in the muscles there. Somewhere he had to find another glow-in-the-dark toothbrush—a pink one, because that was Dani's favorite color. And he had to find a way to talk his daughter out of a trip to the magic dentist, because he wasn't sure if he could stand there and let Samantha Carter pull another silk scarf from his shirt pocket.

He wondered what kind of magic she used to make that little jolt of awareness shoot through him when her fingertips flitted across his chest for all of half a second. Something from her bag of tricks? He wanted to ask but didn't think it would be wise for him to see her again.

Because he didn't believe in magic, yet he was crazy enough to think he'd seen a shooting star on the ceiling in her office today. Joe had almost asked her about the special paint. But she'd think he was nuts, that it was no wonder his son pulled little girls' teeth on the playground and kept them in a jelly jar in the top of his closet.

Joe shook his head and indulged in the chance to swear out loud, because the kids were asleep.

He was going to stay far, far away from Samantha Carter.

Wandering through the house, he picked up things here and there. Dani's shoes and dirty socks that made a trail from the hallway to the living room. As usual she'd kicked them off while she made her way from one room to the next. No amount of talking made the least bit of difference about that particular bad habit of hers.

Luke's book bag from school was on the kitchen table, and Joe dug the lunch box out of the book bag so he could discard whatever Luke hadn't finished of his lunch. Too many times Joe had forgotten, and the mess that confronted him inside the lunch box on a Monday morning was something he could do without.

Inside the book bag, he also found Luke's jacket and two sheets of math problems due tomorrow, all of them wadded into a neat little ball. Maybe they could smooth out the math sheets enough that Luke could turn them in.

As Joe picked up the book bag to put it away, he realized it weighed more than it should have. There was something else inside it.

A rock? That was Joe's first thought. Luke loved rocks. For some reason, he didn't think they had enough of them here, so he collected them at school and brought them home with him.

He unzipped pockets one by one until he hit on the one that held something long and thin and heavy. Joe's fingers closed around it and drew it out of the book bag.

"Dammit, Luke," he said.

In his hand was the tooth-fairy figurine he'd found Luke admiring in the lobby of Samantha Carter's office when Joe had gone to get him. She had long blond hair, a blue dress with stars and a magic wand with fairy dust streaming after it. Luke must have swiped the figurine while Joe was settling the bill.

Which meant Joe would have to see Samantha again.

He tested out his feelings on the subject. He was

not happy. He refused to be. So what if the woman was gorgeous and somehow looked as vulnerable as a fairy who'd gotten her wings singed? So what if touching her, in the simplest of ways, had the power to make him tremble like an overeager teenage boy.

He wasn't going to do anything about it. He couldn't. He had his kids to think about. Kids who'd cried themselves to sleep too many nights to count over a woman who was never coming back to them, one he suspected didn't give them a second thought these days.

No woman was ever going to hurt them again. Joe would see to it.

That meant Samantha Carter was off-limits. He and Luke would take the fairy back and be done with the woman.

Samantha didn't even get a chance to catch her breath until well past noon. A member of the office staff was kind enough to make a run to the nearby sandwich shop and take orders, so Samantha had a turkey sandwich on whole wheat, a diet soda and all of five minutes to down both before her next patient would be ready for her.

Leaning back into the big leather chair, she let the sandwich sit there on her desk, let the soda get warm and go flat. Feeling altogether out of sorts today, she swiveled around in her chair and gave in to the need to let herself think about Joe Morgan and his adorable son.

They were all she'd heard about today. It seemed they'd charmed the entire office staff, and Samantha had given herself away half-a-dozen times when she'd been teased about Mr. Morgan, Sr. He was so polite.

He had a delicious Texas drawl. He was not married anymore. He didn't seem at all caught up in his own charms, an affliction that tended to absolutely ruin most truly good-looking men. She'd gotten those choice bits of gossip within the first five minutes of arriving in the office. By noon someone had started a pool that had grown to twenty-five dollars already. The bet—how long it would be before he called back.

"Am I that transparent?" Samantha complained, when she was closeted in her office at twelve-thirty with her forty-something, normally no-nonsense office manager, Dixie, who'd just given her the latest update on the pool.

"It's the first time I've seen you really smile at anyone over twelve in six weeks. We've been worried about you, sweetie. Besides, he really is cute."

"Lots of men are cute," she argued.

"Not that cute. Besides, I think he's nice, too. I liked the way he talked to his little boy. You can tell everything important about a man by the way he talks to his kids," Dixie claimed.

"If you catch him when no one's listening," Sam said. She'd found many parents who were totally different with their kids when they thought no one was listening. And she certainly hadn't been listening when Richard talked to the girls. She'd missed a great deal there.

"I liked him, and I'm no pushover." Dixie pointed to the turkey on whole wheat and the soda. "And you owe me five and a quarter."

"I'll buy tomorrow?" Sam suggested.

"Fine by me. Unless I win the pot. Then we'll hit that little French place around the corner for some serious take-out."

"Dixie! You got in on this?"

"Of course. I don't suppose you'd like to call him? The bet's good either way. It doesn't matter who makes the call, just as long as the two of you talk."

"No, I'm not going to call him."

"We have his number," she offered. "We even have his address."

"No."

Dixie laughed and headed for the door. "I have to get back to work. My boss is a slave driver."

Samantha sighed and told herself to eat. She didn't have much time. But now she couldn't help herself. She was thinking about the Morgan men, despite all her intentions not to.

Taken individually, either Joe or his son would have caught her interest. Together they were simply devastating. Luke was just too cute, too full of energy and exuberance and shyly given smiles. She'd felt like a great treasure had been bestowed upon her when Luke smiled. Samantha had done her best to put the fear of God into him when it came to working on other children's teeth, but it had been hard to do with Luke practically dancing with excitement and begging her to admit to being the tooth fairy in disguise.

Laughter bubbled up inside her. The tooth fairy?

She wished she was, so she could conjure up whatever Luke wanted so badly. As hard as she'd tried, she hadn't convinced Luke to tell her what that was. She hadn't been able to bring herself to tell him that sometimes wishing simply wasn't enough.

Though she knew little about Luke's situation, she understood quite clearly that Luke needed to believe the magic was real, and she suspected that need came from his wish to have his absent mother back.

Samantha didn't see a lot of dads bring children to her office. She suspected Joe was all Luke had, and that had her wondering if she'd see him again.

It had her thinking of making a fool of herself by pulling a scarf out of his shirt pocket in an effort to make him smile. Joe Morgan looked as if he needed a reason to smile as badly as his son did, and Samantha's first impulse had been to give him one, because she'd wanted to see him smile, too.

Her face burned at the memory of being so foolish as to treat a grown man like a little boy.

It wouldn't have been so bad if Joe hadn't been...well...

Stop it, Samantha, she chastised herself.

So he was good-looking. That didn't mean anything, unless she wanted a man she could simply enjoy looking at from time to time. She couldn't very well sit him in a corner, like a beautiful piece of furniture, or hang him on a wall like a painting and admire him.

So he was charming, in that down-home, straight-off-the-ranch sort of way. Since when did she melt over a man with a Texas accent?

She'd never had a cowboy fantasy in her life, but when she'd closed her eyes the night before, the first thing she saw was a grinning Joe Morgan in a cowboy hat, a dusty pair of jeans and well-worn boots.

Yum, she thought, unable to help herself for a second.

She wasn't even looking for a man. The last thing she wanted or needed was a man. And the absolute last thing she'd allow herself to want or need was a man with kids.

"Samantha?" The voice came from the intercom system on the phone, startling Samantha as it always did when she suddenly found someone speaking to her when she was absolutely alone in the room.

"Yes, Jess," she said.

"Sorry to bother you, but there's a man on the line who said he needs to see you tonight after your last appointment. No emergency. Nothing to do with teeth. And I thought I'd better check with you first before giving him a time. Your last appointment should be over by six."

"Okay." Puzzled, Samantha asked, "Who's the man?"

"Joe Morgan," Jess said innocently. "The would-be dentist's dad."

Samantha couldn't stop a long slow sigh from escaping her mouth.

Obviously Jess heard it, too, because she laughed. "I thought that was him. Which means I win! If he called anytime before two-thirty today, I win!"

"Jess—" she protested.

"I'll put him right through."

The phone buzzed at her, which meant the intercom had been turned off. A light under the button labeled Line 3 started blinking, which meant Joe was there, right at her fingertips.

Samantha closed her eyes and told herself to make up some socially acceptable little lie. She had plans, errands, some reason to get home tonight. But there was nothing. She couldn't lie to herself. She was intrigued. The cute cowboy wanted to see her again. He'd seemed so reluctant to be here yesterday, although it may have been nothing but embarrassment over what his son had done.

If only he knew, Samantha thought. Kids did the

silliest things. Luke certainly wasn't the first or the last to give his father fits.

Samantha took a breath and reached for the receiver. Play it cool, she told herself. He's just a man. Okay, a boyishly handsome man, but one with an adorable kid—definitely off-limits.

She punched the button and said, "Hello? This is Dr. Carter."

"Hi. This is Joe Morgan," he said. "From yesterday? My son—"

"I remember you," she jumped in. As if any woman forgot him. He hesitated then, and she wondered just how eager she'd sounded when she told him she remembered him. Trying to be the professional woman she was supposed to be, Samantha said, "Luke didn't pull another tooth, did he?"

"No. At least, not that anyone's told me about. But the day's still young." Joe might have been smiling then. She couldn't be sure. "I was wondering if Luke and I could come by your office this evening. He has something of yours that he needs to return."

"Oh?"

"I'm afraid he swiped one of your ceramic tooth fairies, Doc."

"He did?" Samantha was surprised and more than a little disappointed now that she knew why he'd called. Despite what she'd told herself about becoming involved with a man like Joe Morgan, a part of her still wanted him to want her enough to call her today. Which was silly, she knew, but that was how she felt.

"I can't believe Luke did that," Joe rushed on. "As far as I know, he's never done anything like that before. I told him he has to return it to you himself so he can explain what he did and tell you how sorry he is. If you could make time for us, of course.''

''Of course,'' she said. ''Six o'clock?''

''That's fine. Thanks.''

''It's no problem at all. Luke is a delightful child.'' She couldn't help but add, ''I hope you won't be too...''

''Harsh?''

''Yes.'' Samantha closed her eyes and winced. It was absolutely none of her business. But Luke was special. She remembered the sad puppy-dog eyes when he'd asked her quite seriously how many teeth she thought it took to get a grand wish granted by the tooth fairy. Not an ordinary wish and certainly not money, he'd explained. A real wish. Real magic.

Oh, Luke. She'd lost a bit of her heart to him already.

''I'm sorry,'' Samantha rushed on. ''I know it's none of my business.''

''It's all right. If it will make you feel better, I'll tell you that I tried to yell at Luke this morning, but I really didn't have the heart to do it,'' Joe admitted. ''Still, he has to know he can't get away with this. And that it's a serious thing to take something that doesn't belong to him.''

''Absolutely,'' Samantha agreed, thinking she should help him out here. ''I'll try to be stern when he apologizes.''

And then she heard this wonderful rich laughter coming through the phone. Joe Morgan was laughing at her, and she couldn't have been more surprised, nor could she imagine such a joyous sound coming out of Joe's mouth. He was altogether too serious.

''You? Stern?'' He laughed again, the sound rolling

over her and sending little shivers of delight along her skin. "You'd be even more hopeless at it than I was."

"W-well," she stammered, all flustered, the room suddenly much too warm, "I could try."

"Okay, Doc," he said. "Give it your best shot."

"I will," she declared, wondering how long it had been since he'd laughed like that.

It had been wonderful to make him laugh. And she wished he'd been here so she could have seen what it did to his face. Half the office staff would have been swooning.

"I'll see you at six," he said, his voice just as deep and sexy as before, a hint of the laughter still there.

"I'll be waiting," she said, then didn't even realize until she'd hung up the phone just how that sounded.

Samantha folded her arms on her desk, then let her head fall into them. She was just so stupid where men were concerned, and she couldn't seem to think before she spoke. She'd have Joe believe that the highlight of her day was going to be his son returning her stolen fairy—which was sad, but true. It would be the best part of her day.

Still, she didn't have to tell Joe that.

Her day flew by from there. With every passing minute, Samantha got more and more nervous. And she knew she was making a fool of herself when she dashed into the washroom at five-thirty and combed her hair and put on some lip gloss. Hers was an all-female office, and every one of her staff members knew exactly who was coming to see her this evening and what she was doing in front of the washroom mirror.

She finished with her last patient at five forty-five, then went into her office and hid. There was paperwork to deal with, but she knew she'd never be able to concentrate on it.

There was nothing to describe how she felt except excited. She was going to see Luke, the little rascal, and Joe. Would Joe smile at her today? Would he open up just a little about what he and Luke were going through? Maybe she could help.

Samantha had all sorts of foolish scenarios running through her head when she heard the intercom buzz.

"Samantha?" said Tess. "You there?"

"Yes." Glancing at her watch, she saw that it was twelve minutes to six. They were early, and she wasn't ready for them. She was too nervous and too hopeful and too foolish for words.

"There's a call for you. Line two. Personal business, I think."

"Thanks, Jess."

Puzzled, Samantha picked up the phone. She didn't have any personal business, had made very few friends in the short time she'd been in Virginia, so she couldn't imagine who this could be.

Unless Joe wasn't coming.

Samantha picked up the phone and said, "Hello."

"Sam?" It was a little girl's voice. "Is that you?"

"Abbie?" Cautious now, she sat back in her chair. In seconds she was all choked up, her eyes brimming with tears. It had been so long since she heard this precious little girl's voice.

"Hi." Abbie sounded relieved for a second.

"Hi, baby." Samantha smiled, finding the moment bittersweet. "How are you?"

"I'm okay," Abbie said tearfully.

"Really?"

"Well—" Abbie hesitated "—maybe not so okay.

I know I'm not supposed to call, but Daddy's not here. And neither is Monica. There's just the baby-sitter, and she thinks you're just a friend of mine from school. So I thought it would be okay. Is it? Okay, I mean?''

"Oh, Abbie." Samantha closed her eyes, and the tears slid down her cheeks. She knew what she had to do, but she wasn't sure how she'd find the courage. The last thing in the world she wanted to do was hurt Abbie. "Did your father tell you not to call me?"

"Yes. But I found the number in his desk drawer, and I thought as long as he didn't know, it would be okay. I miss you, Sam."

"I miss you, too, sweetie. And Sarah. How is she?"

"She's okay, I guess. She's mad that we had to move to a new house just because Monica had to have a bigger one, and she doesn't like her new teacher, but she has a friend in her class. I do, too. The house is big, and it has a great backyard. But there aren't any kids close by. And Daddy's...well, Daddy's okay. Monica is, too, I guess. But...I still miss you so much."

"Abbie, I'm sorry. I love you very much. You know that, don't you? And I always will."

"I don't understand why you had to go so far away."

And Samantha simply couldn't explain it to her, except to say, "You know the worst thing about being a grown-up is that we don't always get to do what we want or to live where we want or to see the people we love as much as we'd like. But I do love you. I won't ever stop. And I love Sarah, too."

"You just don't love Daddy?"

Samantha sighed, then drew in a shaky breath. Richard didn't love *her* anymore. That was the problem. But she couldn't make him the villain here, not to his daughter. Samantha wanted Abbie and Sarah to be happy now with Richard and his new wife, even if it had broken Samantha's heart to lose the girls. And if she wanted the girls to be happy, she couldn't blame their father for what happened.

"Abbie, I'm so sorry. If I could, I'd wave a magic wand and everything would go back to the way it was before, and we'd all be together again."

"But you can do all sorts of magic," Abbie argued. "I saw you. Lots of times. Can't you fix this? So we can be together again?"

"No, sweetie, I can't."

"Well...can I at least call you? When Daddy isn't here? So we can just talk sometimes?"

"Abbie, it's long distance. Your father's going to know you called when he gets the bill and sees my number there."

"He will?"

"I'm afraid so. You're going to have to tell him."

"But he'll get mad."

"Maybe not so mad if you tell him first, Abbie. Tell him you're sorry, and then ask him if it's okay if you call again sometimes. Maybe on my birthday. Do you remember when it is?"

"May?"

"Yes, in May."

"But that's four whole months away! What if I don't want to wait that long? What if I *need* to talk to you?"

Swallowing hard, barely managing to keep her voice steady, Samantha said, "You're going to have to ask your father and do what he says. Because he's your father.''

Whereas, she was nothing to Abbie anymore, at least not according to Abbie's father. Never mind that Samantha spent three years mothering Abbie and Sarah, or that she couldn't love them more if she'd given birth to them.

''Abbie?'' she said softly, working hard not to let the bitterness come through. ''Your father is the one who gets to decide about these things, okay?''

''It's just not fair,'' Abbie said tearfully.

''I know.'' Samantha had to cover the receiver for a minute, because she was crying so hard and she didn't want the little girl to hear. It would only make this harder. ''I love you, sweetie. Tell Sarah I love her, too.''

And then Samantha hung up the phone and wept.

Chapter Three

Joe had no choice but to bring Dani along when he took Luke to Dr. Carter's office. He picked them both up from the late-stay program where they stayed from the time school ended until he got there after work. Then they drove straight to Dr. Carter's, because that was the only way he was going to make it on time.

In the truck Dani had a million questions about where they were going and why. Once she knew Luke was in trouble, she was beside herself with glee. While Joe tried to deal with whatever Luke had done, she danced around Joe, pointing out that *she* hadn't done whatever Luke had.

Joe could be reading Luke the riot act for pulling his sister's hair, and the next thing he knew, Dani would be smiling and chanting, "I didn't pull anyone's hair. I didn't pull anyone's hair," which infuriated Luke even more and didn't do much for Joe's mood, either.

Joe finally decided a bribe was in order, because he didn't want the good doctor to think both his kids were heathens. He told Dani that if she behaved, didn't break anything or steal anything and managed to keep fairly quiet, they would find out where she could get a glow-in-the-dark toothbrush, too.

"Pink?" she said.

Anything, Joe thought. If only she'd behave for the next ten minutes.

"Pink," he said, praying that glow-in-the-dark toothbrushes came in pink and that Dr. Carter could find her one.

They pulled into the parking lot and climbed out of the car, Dani singing a limerick at the top of her lungs that had Luke begging Joe to make her be quiet. Joe had the fairy. Luke was dragging his heels. Joe put his hand at his son's back to propel him toward the door.

"Do y'think she's gonna be really mad?" Luke said, as if that meant much more to him than making his father mad.

"I think she's going to be disappointed that you would take something that didn't belong to you, especially something of hers, because she thought you were her friend."

"Oh." Luke looked even more miserable than before, and his steps had slowed to a crawl.

"It's not going to get any easier," Joe said, holding open the door so Dani could dance through.

"You sure about that?" Luke hung back on the sidewalk.

"Positive." Joe motioned for him to move along. "In. Now. She stayed late tonight to talk to us."

Dani was gazing at the fairies in the display case with the same sort of awe Luke had shown the day before.

"Don't touch anything," Joe warned her as he approached the window to the receptionist desk.

A young woman with reddish hair and a bright smile whom he hadn't noticed the day before was waiting for him. Three more women, all staring at him and smiling, stood behind her.

"Mr. Morgan?" the redhead said.

"Yes." Lord, he was infamous at the dentist's office. His kid pulled teeth and lifted fairies from the waiting room.

All four women smiled at him.

"And this is Luke? And...?"

"His sister, Dani."

Dani turned around and grinned. "Daddy, it's just like in the book! Luke's magic book!"

Joe winced, the legend of the tooth fairy growing ever larger in the minds of his children. "Don't touch anything, sweetheart, okay?"

He turned back to the women, who were still waiting, still smiling. Didn't they have anything to do?

"Samantha's in her office. She's expecting you," the redhead said. "If you'd like to have a word with her first, Luke and Dani can play here for a few minutes. I'd be happy to keep an eye on them."

Joe hesitated. Did he trust himself alone with Dr. Carter again? Maybe she'd pull another scarf out of his shirt pocket. Or explain to him how she made the ceiling glitter like that and how stars came to shoot across the starry sky she'd created in his examination room.

He glanced back at the kids, Dani in awe of the fairy collection, Luke sitting miserably in the corner.

"Don't worry," the woman said. "I have three kids of my own, and dozens come in here every day. I know all the possibilities for trouble in this room."

Joe worked up a smile and tipped his head to her. "Thank you, ma'am. I would like to talk to the dentist."

He told the kids he'd be back shortly, warned them again about behaving, then headed down the hallway grinning like an idiot. He was here to return a piece of stolen property, after all, and to beg for a trick toothbrush for his baby girl.

This in no way resembled a date, even if he *had* tried to take a bath in the sink at the office after work to get rid of the worst of the grime and the sweat clinging to him, then thrown on the clean shirt he tried to remember to keep in the car for those days he was summoned to Luke's school on the way home from work.

Hell, he wouldn't know what a date was, but he for damned sure knew this wasn't the way to make a good first impression on a woman.

Striding down the hall, Joe thought about how much he'd love to get away, thought about the satisfaction he could find planting himself on the back of a horse and riding from dawn to dusk, even eating dust and smelling bad-tempered cows all day.

He missed Texas. He missed working the ranch and being so tired at the end of the day he just fell into bed and didn't so much as blink until the sun was nearly up again and it was time to go to work and do it all over.

It had been another life, he reminded himself, one

he couldn't go back to. Besides, the life he had, while frustrating, even infuriating, at times, wasn't that bad. He had Luke and Dani, and that was forever. No one would ever take them away from him.

And this was all a part of being a parent, Joe told himself.

He'd come here to please his wife; there'd been a time when he'd have done almost anything to make her happy. She'd been pregnant with Luke and uneasy about the whole process and about being a mother, and she'd thought it would be easier having her own mother close by. They couldn't very well keep following the rodeo circuit—not with a newborn baby. It was time to settle down, and they'd settled here in Virginia.

Joe had considered moving back to Texas after Elena left, but this was the only home the kids had ever known, everything that was familiar in their world at a time when so many things had changed. They'd panicked when he'd even mentioned the possibility of moving, and he'd decided to stay put for their sake. They needed all the stability he could offer them at the moment—same school, same friends, same house. And as much as Elena's parents had disapproved of him at first, they'd been great to him since Elena had left. They seemed as baffled by their daughter's behavior as he was, and embarrassed, as well. They were great to his kids and understanding and supportive as Joe fumbled his way through life as a single parent.

He was fumbling right now—over teeth.

Resigned to guiding his son through his apology to the lady dentist, Joe lifted a hand to knock on the door next to the plaque that read Dr. Samantha Carter.

But the door wasn't quite shut, and as he paused in

front of it, he heard something. A muffled strangled sort of sound. Pushing the door open another two inches, he glanced inside and saw the slight figure of a woman hunched over the big desk. Her shoulders were shaking, her head buried in her hands.

Glancing around the office, he saw that she was all alone, and Joe couldn't quite stomach that. Something about a woman crying her heart out, all alone, just didn't sit right with him. He had to help her.

Even as he told himself it was none of his business, that he couldn't let himself touch her, couldn't hold her, he did, anyway. He didn't let himself think about the fact that he barely knew her or about how very much he wanted to hold her.

He pushed open the door, then closed it behind him, because she didn't need an audience right now. She needed a shoulder, someone to hold on to, someone to whisper in her ear some empty meaningless words like "Everything will be all right," and Joe was the only one here. He'd have to do it. No self-respecting gentleman would have left her alone with her tears.

Joe wasn't afraid of those tears. He had three sisters, after all. One of them was always crying. He walked across the room and put his hand on her back. "Doc?"

She froze, caught her breath, then turned around slowly, cautiously, as if she couldn't believe she'd been caught like this. Her eyes were red and glistened with unshed tears. Her nose was a little red, as well. Tear tracks led down her cheeks, giving way to splotches of wetness on her dark blue blouse, and her mouth was trying to work itself into a smile, but failing.

She looked utterly miserable. And adorable. And very kissable.

He wanted to kiss her. That definitely wasn't part of the plan. He was just supposed to make her feel a little better, to hold her until she managed to dry her tears—no kisses involved.

She hung her head, apparently not willing to meet his gaze any longer. Joe dipped his head low and tried to get her to look at him again.

"Wanna tell me what's wrong, Doc?" he invited, making himself comfortable leaning against the side of her desk while she remained seated in that huge chair.

She swiped at her tears, missing half of them in her haste, then couldn't stop more from falling.

"Come on," he said gently, leaning closer, thinking about pulling her into his arms. "You can tell me."

He figured he owed her. After all, she'd made him laugh this morning on the phone. How long had it been since he'd laughed like that? The idea of her being stern with a kid just did him in. It was as hopeless as the idea that he'd be able to leave her alone like this.

No way, he told himself.

She rolled her chair back so she could get away from him, but he slid across the desk until he was right in front of her, half sitting on the edge of it. He leaned over, catching her chair by its arms, then reached for her hands, instead. With one fluid motion he pulled her to him, had her plastered against him and clinging to him, this trembling mass of woman, smelling incredible and feeling like a frightened kitten that needed to be gentled to his touch and taught that she had nothing to fear from him.

He drank in the scent of her, because she did smell very good. And she was a tiny little thing, all silky hair and shaky breaths and tears. They just kept falling.

"Tell me," he said again, knowing she wouldn't feel better until she got it out.

Her face was pressed against his chest, the contact muffling the sound as she whispered to him, "I was just talking to Abbie."

"Abbie?" He stroked her hair and bent down closer. "Who's Abbie?"

"A little girl. A nine-year-old girl. And she was crying and telling me that life just isn't fair. Which I knew already. But why did she have to learn that at nine? Why does any kid?"

"I don't know, Doc." He sighed and tightened his arms around her, because she was still trembling badly.

He should have known this had something to do with a kid in trouble. Any woman who went to so much trouble to help little children not to be so afraid at the dentist obviously had a major soft spot where kids were concerned.

He wondered just what this Abbie was to her. Obviously she cared about the little girl very much. "Tell me about Abbie."

"She lives in Seattle and I haven't seen her in months. And I miss her so much," Samantha whispered.

Joe held her through the worst of it, until her sobs subsided and the trembling ceased, until he felt some warmth come back into her and then tension as she became aware of exactly where she was and who she was with.

He felt her stiffen in his arms, felt her pull away slightly, then saw her staring at him as if she was suddenly afraid. Then she couldn't get away fast enough. Color flooded her cheeks and she jumped back, hitting her chair. She probably would have fallen if his hands hadn't shot out and grabbed her again.

"Steady," he said. "I don't bite."

Warily she dried her eyes and curled her bottom lip over her bottom row of teeth. If she even came close to gnawing on that delectable lower lip of hers, he was going to stop her.

By kissing her.

He'd take that lip of hers between his for safekeeping.

Samantha pushed a stray hair behind her ears and looked around the room as if she needed to reassure herself that she truly was in her own office, that this really happened.

"I'm so sorry," she began, then just stood there with her mouth hanging open.

It made him think of kissing her again, which no gentleman would do right now, because that would clearly be taking advantage of her. And Joe had always thought of himself as a gentleman.

But he was tempted. So tempted.

Flustered, Samantha straightened her coat, then her hair again, then wiped her face dry. "I'm sorry."

"It's all right, Doc. It's your office. You can cry all you want."

Color flooding her cheeks again, she reached for him, her fingertips brushing past chest. "I got your shirt all wet."

He sucked in a breath and fought the urge to catch her hand and hold it there against him. "The shirt's been wet before. No harm done."

"I'm sorry." She looked utterly miserable and embarrassed and at a loss for anything else to say.

Joe decided the woman was in dire need of someone to take care of her, to watch over her and fuss over her and reassure her a little. Wasn't there anyone around to do that for her?

He reached for her hand and held it in both of his. Her palm was flat against his, his other hand stroking the back of hers. "Who do you go home to at the end of the day, Doc?"

"I used to go home to Felix," she mumbled, tugging her hand from his.

"Felix?" He certainly didn't sound like much competition.

"He's a dog."

"A real one?" Joe asked hopefully. "Or the kind who walks on two legs?"

She laughed a little then. "Four legs, wags his tail—a real dog."

"That's it? A dog?"

She nodded.

"You don't even have him anymore?"

"No," she said sadly.

"No family?" He knew her father had died recently, but surely there was someone else.

"No one," she said, the look on her face making him want to haul her back into his arms.

"No man in your life?"

"Not anymore."

"No kids?"

She shook her head and turned to look at the painting on the wall to the right, and Joe thought of Abbie. Who was Abbie?

"Well, Doc, sounds like you need a friend."

She opened her mouth to say something, then obviously thought better of it and closed it again. He watched her waffling back and forth on just what she was going to say, watched the silence make her more and more uncomfortable.

Finally she said, "I haven't been in town that long."

"It's a friendly town," Joe said, aching to touch her again even in the smallest of ways.

"I'm sure it is." She turned her wrist over, so she could see the time on that dainty gold watch of hers. "Oh, I'm sorry. I'm sure I'm keeping you from…something. Where's Luke?"

"In the waiting room. I thought I'd let him sweat it out a minute before he makes his apology. And I should warn you—my daughter's here, too."

She hesitated, looking scared again. "You have a daughter?"

He nodded. "Dani. She's four. She's so jealous of Luke's glow-in-the-dark toothbrush she can hardly stand it. I promised her we'd find her one somewhere."

"Oh, no problem. I buy them by the case." She put her hand into the big pockets of her white coat and pulled out a handful of stuff.

He saw scarves in three different colors, coins, thick tongue depressors and a set of plastic teeth. Picking them up, he turned the crank and they started dancing along the desktop.

Joe laughed, as he had this morning, while Samantha fished in the other pocket until she came up with two toothbrushes.

"Pink or purple?" she asked.

"Pink, definitely. What else have you got in those pockets?"

"Tricks of the trade," she said. "Anything to make the kids smile."

And then Joe simply couldn't resist her anymore. Stepping close, tucking her hair behind her ear, then brushing his knuckles against the side of her face, he said, "Who makes you smile, Doc?"

Her eyes got so big and so blue, and she seemed to stop breathing all together. "No one," she said softly. "Not for a long time."

"I think it's time someone did." He brushed the pad of his thumb across her bottom lip.

She exhaled shakily, her breath skimming across his thumb. Joe caught her face between both hands. Ready to take his time, to savor the moment, because he hadn't wanted to kiss a woman so much in a long, long time, he started at her eyes, kissing them softly, finding them still wet from her tears. The skin of her cheek was soft, and the tip of her nose was cold. He kissed all of those spots as his hands tangled in her hair.

She relaxed a little against him, her hands landing flat against his back, then hanging on to him, pulling him a little closer. Joe lowered his mouth to hers and teased at her lips with his tongue. Then he drew that lower lip into his mouth and nibbled on it a bit.

She moaned, the soft sexy sound coming from deep inside her.

He wasn't doing this because he'd come in here and found her crying or because he wanted to see her smile or because the loneliness radiated from her like light shining from the lamp in the corner. He was doing it because he had to have a taste of her, had to crush her against him and see if this kiss was anywhere near as good as he imagined it would be.

She whimpered a little and leaned into him when he set her bottom lip free and made a desperate grab for air before he stopped teasing her and kissed her for real. Her lips parted easily for his. Her hands, which had settled near his waist, near his hips, urged him closer as her whole body opened up to his and she simply melted against him. She tasted so sweet. He stroked her mouth with his tongue, groaned a little when he felt her breasts crush against his chest and felt the dizzying swirl of desire racing through him.

"Mmm," she moaned when he came up for air again.

It felt so good. Nothing had felt this good to him in the longest time. And he wanted to—

"Dad! Dani's bugging me!" Luke bellowed, then came charging into the room, tripping over his own two feet just inside the door and not seeming to notice anything that was going on in the room. He righted himself and then proceeded to launch into his list of complaints. "I'm making a tower with the blocks and she keeps knocking it down. And then I tried to make her leave me alone and she started to cry!"

Joe took his time stepping away from Samantha, and he had to remind himself that he loved his son very much, even if the little urchin had the manners of a savage. Try as he might, he couldn't seem to teach Luke to knock on a closed door, to go find someone, instead of yelling, when he wanted to talk to the person or to respect anyone's privacy.

Samantha looked mortified and so sad, so kissable. He could still taste her on his lips. *Damn.*

"Will you come'n make her leave me alone, Dad? Please?"

"Luke, that's a door," Joe said, pointing it out to his son, in case Luke missed it. "It's the door to Dr. Carter's office, and it was closed. What does that mean you should do?"

"But Dani was bugging me!"

"Luke," he warned.

"Knock, okay? I should knock. Sorry."

"Don't tell me. Tell her." He nodded toward Samantha. "And while you're at it—" he dug into his pocket and came up with the pretty fairy "—give her this and see if you can explain what you did and why. I'll go find your sister and deal with her."

"'Kay," Luke said miserably, sighing as he took the fairy into his hand.

"Dani and I'll be waiting out front," he said, then allowed himself one more look at Samantha. Her cheeks were flushed, her lips a little swollen, her breath coming in quick little bursts.

Joe winked at her, which had soft color flooding her cheeks once again and making her look even more kissable than ever. Damn.

As he turned to go, he realized she still hadn't told him who Abbie was or why she missed the little girl so much. And he still hadn't managed to make Samantha smile.

Samantha's head was spinning, for reasons she simply couldn't understand.

All he'd done was kiss her. It wasn't as though she'd never been kissed. But then, she'd never kissed Joe Morgan. Could it make that much difference which man did the kissing?

Perplexed, her spinning head making her dizzy, Samantha concentrated on Luke Morgan, cute as ever and looking absolutely miserable as he stood in front of her, clutching her favorite fairy figurine to his chest.

He didn't say anything for the longest time, just scuffed one of his sneakers against the other and sighed big heavy sighs. Finally he held the fairy out to her.

"I took it," he said. "Yesterday, when I was here. But I didn't mean to keep it. Honest, I didn't. I just had to take it home for a little while."

"Why, Luke?"

"I had to see if it was the one, if she was the fairy in the book, and she was. That's all I had to see. I didn't hurt her a bit. An' I'm real sorry I took her, 'cause my dad's so mad at me."

"Luke?" He was so sweet and so worried she had to fight not to smile. "Is that why you're sorry? Because your dad found out what you did and he got mad?"

Luke puzzled over that for a moment, as if it might be a trick question. "Well," he admitted, "I am sorry he found out. And that he's mad. But…I'm not s'pposed to take things that don't belong to me. Is that what I'm s'pposed to be sorry about?"

Samantha couldn't help it. She smiled, then started to laugh, then felt all the tension leave her body as she hugged Luke close, then kissed him on the forehead, something he endured without too much protest, although she could see she'd probably insulted his sense of dignity. After all, he was seven.

Still smiling brightly, Samantha said, "I think you know what you did wrong, Luke."

"I really am sorry," he said. "I liked it here and I liked you. Are you really mad at me?"

"I think I can forgive you," she said.

"And you'll still gimme my wish?" he asked earnestly.

"Wish?"

"You don't have to pretend with me," he whispered, then looked around as if to see if anyone was listening. "I know who you are."

"You do?"

"Yeah. I recognized you from when you came to my school that day in your real clothes."

"Real clothes?" Oh, no. Samantha knew what was coming next.

"You're the tooth fairy! I know 'cause you look just like the one in my magic book. An' I saw you do the magic, too! Tell me you're not really mad. Tell me you're still gonna gimme my wish."

Samantha got down on her knees in front of him and told herself not to ask. It was none of her business, and he wasn't her kid. Much as she might wish for someone just like him in her life, there was no one. And she'd promised herself she'd never fall in love with another man's kids again.

It was too much of a risk. If she came to love Luke, as she'd loved Abbie and Sarah, then lost him, she simply wouldn't survive it this time.

"Please," said the precious little boy, near tears now.

Bracing herself, she ignored the whole argument about her magical powers and asked, "What do you want, Luke?"

"My mom," he said solemnly. "I want her to come back."

Samantha stared at him, unable to say anything.

"Can you do it?" Luke asked with absolute sincerity. "I know you can. You have to, 'cause nobody else would."

Samantha shook her head, trying to clear it so she could think. "What do you mean, no one else would?"

"Santa didn't do it. And I wished on my birthday candles, but that didn't work. I wished on a star and a four-leaf clover, but that didn't work, either. But I didn't know about you, then. I didn't understand that the magic is real. And then I saw you do it, and I knew you were the one. I knew you could bring my mom back for me. So will you?"

"Luke," she began, then looked around in hopes that Joe might come back. Honestly, this wasn't anything for her to handle. This was Joe's son, Joe's problem. It was none of her business.

"I know I don't have all the teeth yet, but I'm working on it. I thought a hundred would do it."

"A hundred!" She nearly shrieked. "A hundred baby teeth?"

Luke nodded solemnly, and Samantha had to sit down. She took one of the smaller chairs pulled to the front of her desk, and Luke sat down in the other, as if they were going to negotiate some business between them here in Samantha's office.

"Is a hundred enough?" Luke asked. "I only have six now, but I've got two loose teeth. See?" He opened up his mouth and wiggled two of his teeth with his tongue. "And I know three other kids in my class who have loose teeth, too. One of 'em's already promised me his for fifty cents and a really cool T-rex sticker I got at the zoo."

Samantha just sat there with her mouth hanging open, not knowing how to begin to explain this to him.

"T-rex is a dinosaur," Luke explained.

"Oh, Luke," Samantha said, then simply didn't know what to add.

Luke must have known something was wrong, because he looked near tears again. "You're not gonna do it, are you?"

"No. I mean, I'm not refusing to do it. I just...I have to talk to your father, Luke."

"I already asked him to bring her back, and he wouldn't."

"He wouldn't? Or he couldn't? It's not the same thing, Luke."

The little boy was crying now. Samantha got down on her knees in front of him and pulled him into her arms. Skinny little arms crept around her neck, and his tears soaked into her collar as he hung on for dear life, much in the same way she'd hung on to Joe earlier.

She couldn't help but think of Abbie then. Somewhere, nearly three thousand miles away, Abbie was crying, too, because she loved Samantha like a mother, and Samantha was gone. Samantha worried that there wasn't anybody to hold Abbie when she cried, so she made her arms even tighter around Luke.

Two kids, she thought. Two mothers gone.

She wouldn't judge Luke's mother too harshly, not without hearing from the woman herself about what happened. Because Samantha knew what it was like to have a child wrenched away.

Surely there was nothing worse in the world.

She wondered what sort of explanation Richard had given his girls for her leaving, wondered if he'd made her out to be the bad guy in all of this. She had certainly tried not to make him the villain in front of the girls, because he and his new wife were all the girls had left.

And now Samantha wondered what had happened between Joe Morgan and his wife. She remembered when she and Joe had talked in her office yesterday.

"What does Luke want?" she'd asked him. *"Something that's not within your power to give?"*

Still, he hadn't said whether he couldn't bring Luke's mother back or whether he didn't want to. There was a difference. Samantha wondered why Luke's mother might refuse to come home; that was a possibility, too, that his mother simply wouldn't come home. And she wondered why a kid as wonderful as Luke had to be standing here in Samantha's arms sobbing his little heart out and plotting and scheming to get his hands on a hundred baby teeth to get his mother back.

Life was so strange, she thought. And so very sad.

But it shouldn't be. Especially not for little children like Luke.

Chapter Four

Joe waited for five minutes while Dani danced around the waiting room. In the space of those five minutes, she'd already asked him ten times about the glow-in-the-dark toothbrush. She was the most impatient creature he'd ever encountered, even more impatient than his ex-wife. And that, Joe knew, was saying something.

He was impatient to know what was going on between Luke and Samantha, to know whether she was mad at Joe about that kiss, now that she'd had a chance to think about it.

He wondered exactly what had possessed him to do something so impulsive, something so dangerous, as kissing a woman the way he had.

He'd promised himself that he would keep his relationships with women simple and straightforward from now on. He had his kids to think about, after all. Nobody got to hurt his kids again.

But Samantha Carter wasn't the kind of woman he could keep away from his kids, not if he was involved with her, which he couldn't be.

Still, he hadn't been able to resist trying to comfort her when she cried, hadn't been able to keep his lips off hers when she'd been so sad and sweet, so tempting.

Joe swore softly.

"Daddy, did you say a bad word?"

Joe winced, then apologized to his daughter. "Let's go find Luke," he said.

"And my toof-bwush?"

"Of course. Your toothbrush."

"She really has a pink one for me?"

"Yes, she does."

"Wow!" Dani said, pulling open the door and taking off at a run before Joe could stop her.

"Dani? Wait for me. You don't even know where you're going." He took off after her.

"I found the star room!" she exclaimed.

Sure enough, she had. The blue room with the glittering stars in the painted sky was right there. Joe reached inside and flicked on the light, which bounced off the stars, setting them off and making them seem to twinkle in a way Joe couldn't understand at all.

"Wow!" Dani said again, her eyes big now. "Luke said it was magic, and it is."

It had to be glitter, Joe thought. A woman who walked around with pockets full of chattering teeth would glue glitter to her ceiling to please the children reclining in the dental chair.

"Come on, Dani. We need to find Luke."

She skipped down the hall, singing as she went, her hair bouncing behind her. The child had more energy than any seven human beings put together. Like that silly pink bunny on the battery commercials, she kept going and going and going.

"To the right, Dani," he said, directing her to the office. She pushed her way inside without a knock or a word to the owner of said office. Par for the course, Joe decided. Privacy was a concept totally unknown to his children.

"Luke's crying," Dani announced as Joe walked through the open door of Samantha's office.

Frowning, he saw that Luke had indeed been crying. Samantha had, as well, but he couldn't tell if it had been fifteen minutes ago, when Joe was here holding her, or more recently, when she was talking to Luke.

What the hell happened? He had very little patience or even the ability to reason when it came to his kids getting hurt. He was all they had now, and he shot her a burning look.

"Are you going to help me?" Luke cried to Samantha.

"Luke...I have to talk to your father first."

Luke glared at her, but his lower lip was trembling, diminishing the effect.

"You're right. We need to talk," Joe said, flashing back to all the times in the past thirteen months he'd seen his son in tears over another woman, a woman who had all but torn out his heart.

He tried to calm down and not glare at Samantha, knowing he was madder than he had a right to be, considering he had no idea what had gone on in this room.

She wouldn't hurt his son, he told himself. He

would have sworn he knew the kind of woman she was and that she wouldn't hurt Luke. Of course, he never would have believed Elena would walk out on his kids, either.

Maybe he just didn't know anything when it came to women. That was a possibility, Joe decided. That was reason enough to stay away from them, or at least to keep them away from his kids.

Looking at Luke, he just couldn't believe this was happening. Luke was devastated. What in the world went on in here?

"Do you really have a toof-bwush for me?" Dani jumped in.

Samantha turned to his daughter and smiled. "If you're Dani, I do. Pink?"

Dani nodded happily. When Samantha pulled the prize pink brush from her pocket, she took it and asked, "Does it really glow?"

"Yes, it does."

"I gotta test it." Dani's eyes scanned the room, then settled on the door in the corner, which most likely led to a closet. She and Luke had played and played in one of the closets at the house the night before with Luke's toothbrush.

"Dani, wait a minute," Joe said, too harshly. "You can't just go into someone else's closet."

"Why not?" She pouted.

Joe winced. He was too worried about Luke to get into it with Dani right now.

"We need to talk later," Samantha said. When he turned to face her, she mouthed to him, "Without the children."

Joe nodded, but wondered if he could wait that long. He wanted some answers. Now.

"I'll call you tonight," she said.

He took Dani by the hand, despite her protests about not being ready to go. Luke threw one more pleading look in Samantha's direction, then turned and left.

Joe thought Samantha looked as if she was going to cry again, and he wanted to hit something. What in the world had she said to Luke?

Luke didn't say anything on the way home. He didn't eat his dinner, raced through his homework, didn't even want to play Nintendo.

Joe was absolutely baffled, and if Samantha Carter didn't call him soon, he was going to break something in two. Maybe a nice piece of crystal, he thought, the stuff his wife had paid a fortune for. She'd been sure they'd have a need for such frivolous extravagances eventually. They never had.

Well, maybe she did now, but she hadn't bothered to pack the stuff she'd picked out when she was living with him. She'd left behind a lot, including two frightened little children.

One of those children was hiding in the linen closet with her pink toothbrush, which did indeed glow in the dark. The other was nowhere to be found. Joe searched the whole house, calling out Luke's name as he went. He was starting to get really worried when Dani stuck her head out of the closet and yelled, "He's in the closet in his room, Daddy!"

He stuck his head in the door. "You could have told me before I searched the entire house, Dani."

"I thought you'd find him," she said innocently. Then added gleefully, "Is Luke in trouble?"

"I'll let you know once I find him," Joe said.

Joe headed upstairs, walked into Luke's room, then knocked on the closet door.

"Who is it?" a muffled voice called out.

"Your father. Can I come in? Please?"

The door opened. Joe got down on his knees and found Luke hiding in a tangle of dirty clothes that somehow never made it to the clothes hamper. They lived here in Luke's closet until he had nothing to wear, and Joe finally came to see why.

Luke had made a nest of the clothes, hunkering down inside the pile clutching his flashlight and a jar.

"Can I sit there?" Joe indicated a spot to his son's right.

Luke shrugged and said, "'Kay."

Joe sat. "Want to tell me what's wrong?"

"Uh-uh."

Joe saw that Luke had the jelly jar with the baby teeth in it. "Pretty impressive collection," he said, taking the jar from Luke's hands.

Luke grabbed it back. "It's mine."

"Sorry." Joe decided to back off. "Luke, I wish you'd tell me what's wrong. I might be able to help."

"You won't," Luke said.

Joe leaned down so he could look his son in the eye. "Hey, partner. I would do anything in the world for you. Don't you know that?"

Luke's bottom lip started to quiver. His whole face puckered, his little nose scrunched up like a cat's, and he began to sob. Joe pulled his son into his arms and for the second time that day, let someone cry all over his favorite shirt for reasons he didn't understand and wasn't likely to hear.

He'd never really found out what had upset Samantha, either, he remembered.

* * *

Samantha had Luke's address in her patient file at the office, and she copied that down before she left. She went to her house, but was too nervous to stay there. She expected an angry phone call from Richard after the conversation she had with Abbie today, and she wasn't up to dealing with Richard tonight. She felt too fragile, her feelings rubbed raw, all the old hurts exposed.

Looking at Joe's little girl had taken her back to another time, when Abbie was Luke's age and Sarah had been so much like Dani. She'd ached to hold Joe's daughter close, but knew he wouldn't have allowed it this evening.

Joe had been angry when he found Luke crying in Samantha's office, and there simply hadn't been a way to explain quickly or privately what Luke wanted. So she decided she'd have to go and see him tonight. He had a right to know what was going on with Luke. She couldn't leave him totally unaware of the fact that his kid was going to try to collect one hundred baby teeth in a jar and trade them for a mother.

In the car she took out her map, because she still didn't know a lot about the city, and drove for about three miles before she found Joe's house. It was in an older neighborhood, a narrow but deep two-story house with all sorts of bushes and big trees, toys scattered here and there, a pretty swing on the porch. It looked lived-in, Samantha decided. She liked it, just as she liked Joe and Luke and Dani.

Getting out of the car, she studied the front of the house and found the bedrooms dark, but lights on downstairs. That was good. She wanted to wait until the kids were asleep so she and Joe could talk privately.

Samantha hadn't quite decided what she was going to say to him. Walking to the door, she ignored the doorbell and knocked quietly, instead. No one answered, and she knocked again, more forcefully this time.

"Coming," she heard Joe call.

Then the door swung open and he stood there, wearing nothing but a fresh pair of jeans and a towel slung over one shoulder. His hair was wet, and he smelled all clean and new. When he propped one of his arms against the door frame and leaned into it, the light from the porch fell across his chest, and the sight made her mouth go dry. She forgot everything she'd said about needing to keep her distance from this man, particularly about staying out of his arms.

He had one of those all-over tans, the kind that didn't seem to fade in the winter at all, and he wasn't that big or that broad, but beautifully made. They could teach anatomy using a body like this, she decided, looking at his sleekly muscled chest and shoulders, the narrow waist, and the rest of him, inside those soft well-worn jeans that fit him like a second skin.

"I probably shouldn't have come here," she said stupidly.

Probably? she mused. *As if there was any question?*

He reached out and snagged her arm. "Well, you're here, Doc, and you're going to tell me what had my son so upset this evening."

"He wouldn't tell you?" she asked, letting him pull her inside and shut the door behind her.

"No. He hid in his closet with that jar of teeth he's

collecting and cried until bedtime. He didn't tell me a damned thing, but you will.''

Samantha stepped away from him and found her back pressed against the wall. Joe protecting his children was something to behold. Obviously no one was going to mess with his kids without hearing about it from him. It only made her like him more.

''That's why I came over here,'' she said. ''To tell you.''

He folded his arms across his chest, seeming perfectly at ease with the fact that he was only half-dressed and totally oblivious to the effect that had on her. Right then he was totally focused on his son.

Good, Samantha thought. She would focus on Luke, as well. After all, that was why she was here.

''Could we sit down?'' she said, thinking she might put some distance between him and her, that the distance might somehow diminish the power he had over her.

He gave her a look that said she was pushing her luck by stalling this way, but stepped away and nodded toward the sofa. It was a buttery soft leather, expensive, and not what she would have expected from a man like him. She would have thought his tastes ran to simpler things.

Glancing around the room, she saw it was done with equally expensive taste, the effect of its quality pieces, obviously chosen with the help of a decorator, softened somewhat by the tiny shoes piled in the corner by the door, the coats thrown across the big leather chair in the corner, the toys scattered here and there throughout the room.

Samantha sat on one end of the sofa and ran her hand along the arm.

"My wife," Joe said. "She liked expensive things."

"Oh," Samantha said softly. *"Liked?"*

"Hmm?"

"You said *liked*. Not *likes*. Does she still like expensive things? Or is she…"

"I wouldn't know what she likes anymore. I haven't seen her in thirteen months. Did Luke talk to you about his mother?"

"A little." This was going to be more difficult than Samantha realized, and she was nervous. "I know this isn't any of my business, but…why did Luke's mother go away?"

"Because deep down inside, where it really matters, she's selfish and immature, and being a mother to two little kids was just too hard for her. It wasn't fun anymore, not when it called for putting the happiness and the needs of two little children ahead of her own."

His tone was dead even as he said it, although from the tension she saw come into his shoulders and the hard line of his jaw, she suspected Joe Morgan was bitterly angry about what he'd just told her.

Selfish? she thought. Immature? How did he ever get tangled up with a woman like that?

If she truly was a woman like that. Samantha didn't know that for sure. She barely knew this man, she reminded herself. She couldn't afford to take every word he said as gospel. She couldn't give any man's word that much credibility, not ever again.

"I'm sorry," she said. "I know it's none of my business, but—"

"It's all right. And it's not all her fault. I married her. I had children with her, without ever seeing what she was truly like. It's my fault, too."

"You're not the one who ran out on your kids," she pointed out.

"No," he said. "I could never do that."

"And she could?" Samantha found that difficult to believe.

He shrugged, the gesture holding a world of hurt. "Elena was indulged her whole life. Her parents have a lot of money. They made things easy for her. She always got whatever she wanted, and at some point, she decided she wanted me. I think I was part of the shock-your-parents phase, because at the time I didn't have much more than I could fit in the back of the camper I was hauling behind my truck, and most all I ever did was follow the rodeo from one town to another."

"You?" she said.

Joe nodded. "Elena went through a phase in the middle of her college education where she wanted to be a photographer. She came to take pictures of the rodeo one night, and one thing kind of led to another. Next thing I knew, she was in the truck with me and off we went. One rodeo after another. Her parents hated it."

"I can imagine," Samantha said.

"She was a lot of fun back then. We had a lot of fun together, and for a while that was enough for me. I liked to have fun. But we all have to grow up sometime. For me, it was when she got pregnant with Luke. The rodeo just didn't cut it anymore. Texas wasn't that appealing to her, either. We got married, came to Virginia to tell her parents, and somehow we ended up staying here. I think she thought her daddy would step in and make everything all better then."

"Better?"

"Money," Joe said as if it was a dirty word. "We needed a house, one she approved of. And furniture and all kinds of baby things. I think Elena believed her father would cough up enough for all that. But he didn't, and even if he had, I wouldn't have taken it. He did offer me a job in his electronics firm, which I wasn't at all qualified for and also refused to take."

"Which didn't sit well with Luke's mother?"

"No," he said. "She might have forgiven her father and me for the house. Or the lack of a house she approved of. But she got pretty steamed over the job offer I refused and all the money that came with it. We settled in here…" He glanced around the little house. "She grew up in a mansion. Or what I think of as a mansion. And this place…well, it's in great shape now, compared to what it was when we first bought it. I'd done some construction work before, and I took a job with a local builder, worked on this place on the side. Luke came along. Things were a little rocky, and then Dani came along. And that's when it got really tough."

"Two kids are a lot of work," Samantha sympathized.

Joe didn't look a bit forgiving. "I know."

"So what happened?"

"I think it was just too hard for Elena. Too much work for her. I mean, the money was part of it. She always resented the fact that we didn't have as much as she thought we should, or that I wouldn't work for her father, or that her parents wouldn't give her more. But mostly I think she had no idea what she was getting into by having kids. You said it, it's a lot of work."

Samantha nodded. "It's unrelenting."

"Yeah. And Elena still wanted to have fun, to spend money, to see her friends. There wasn't a lot of time for that with two kids. She was miserable, and I shouldn't be so bitter about the fact that she left. She never would have been happy here, and the kids would have known that in time. She would have made them miserable, too. It never would have worked. I know that. It's just hard as hell to explain to a kid who's lost his mother."

"I'm sorry," Samantha said.

"Well, now you know. And I guess I owe you an apology, too. I see red at the thought of another woman hurting my son. He's cried himself to sleep too many nights already, and I...I'm afraid I was a little rough on you today, Doc."

"It's all right."

"It's just that I'm all they've got left," Joe said. "The only one left to protect them and take care of them."

"I understand. I'd growl at anybody who hurt them, too."

"Thank you," he said, relaxing just a bit for the first time since he'd found Luke sobbing in her office. "So what did Luke tell you?"

"He wants his mother back."

Joe turned his head to the side and swore. Samantha flinched at the raw power and the anger behind the carefully controlled words.

"I can't make her come back," he admitted. "No matter how much Luke wants her."

"Of course. I didn't mean that you could. Or that you should. I was just telling you what he told me. And, Joe?"

"Hmm?"

"Luke has this ridiculous idea that I'm the tooth fairy, because he saw me in that silly costume I wear when I talk to kids at schools, and now he's decided I can bring his mother back to him. He's trying to collect a hundred teeth in that jar of his so he can use them to make a grand gesture to the tooth fairy in exchange for getting his mother back."

"Oh, God," Joe said, looking like he'd had the breath knocked out of him. "A hundred teeth?"

Samantha nodded.

"Well, that's a problem."

"I know. I tried to tell him I wasn't really magic, but he saw me do those silly little magic tricks, and now he thinks I can do anything. That's why he's so mad at me—he thinks I could bring his mother back if I wanted to, that I just won't do it."

Joe sighed and shook his head. "Luke thinks the same thing about me—that I could bring her back, too."

"I'm sorry." She gave his hand a little squeeze, and when she would have pulled away, he turned his over and captured hers. "And sorry for giving him all these ideas about magic. For going off to school in that silly costume, pulling magic coins from behind the kids' ears and talking to them about magic and fairies. I can't believe I still do that."

"I think it's cute," he said, that teasing smile of his returning, the charm coming on full force along with it. "I'd love to see you in your fairy suit. Why do you do it, Doc?"

"It's silly," she argued.

"So is all-out war waged with water guns and making mud pies and kissing Dani's favorite doll good-night, but I do it, because it makes my kids happy. That's why you do the tooth-fairy bit, isn't it?''

''Part of the reason.''

''Tell me,'' he said, easing back against the cushions, the leather creaking and settling as he did so.

''It was my father's idea. He always went to schools to talk to kids about taking care of their teeth, but they didn't always listen that well. So he decided he needed to spice up his act. And he started doing little magic tricks, and that worked. Then, one year for Halloween, I wanted to be the tooth fairy. And my mother made me this wonderful dress with stars on it and found me a magic wand and a wig with long blond hair, because mine was short at the time. And I had a blast. My father thought I looked perfect, and he had this idea to take me along with him the next time he spoke to a group of kids.

''So we did it. And he told them I was the tooth fairy and that they would make me happy if they would just take good care of their teeth.'' She smiled, seeing her father now. ''He said it was the best audience of first graders he'd ever had. And from then on he took me with him whenever he did his little talks.''

Joe laughed, that wonderful laugh from today on the phone. Lord, she thought, it made her feel good when he laughed.

''We worked up an act,'' she continued, ''like a magician and his assistant. It was one of those special father/daughter things for us. I was still going to schools with him when I was in college.''

''He sounds like a wonderful father.''

''He was.'' She couldn't keep the tears from pooling in her eyes, but was determined not to cry this time. If she did, Joe might well take her in his arms again, and she couldn't let that happen.

"You still miss him very much, don't you."

She nodded.

"I wonder if it ever stops. I wonder if Luke will ever stop missing his mother and asking me to bring her back."

"She doesn't have anything to do with the children?"

He shook his head. "Packed her things and left. She doesn't even call and ask about them."

"And what have you told the kids about why she left?"

"As little as possible," Joe said. "Hell, at first I was sure she didn't mean anything she said when she left. I was sure she'd come to her senses and come back. And even when she said she wouldn't, I had to keep hoping for the kids' sake that she'd change her mind. But it's been more than a year now. The only time I heard from her was when she wanted a divorce, which I gave her. I can't lie to myself anymore. She's not coming back."

"I'm sorry," Samantha said again as Joe slid across the sofa until he was sitting next to her, his right arm lying along the back of the cushion. It would be so easy for him to wrap his arms around her, she thought.

No one had held her in the longest time. Surely that was why it felt so good to be close to him this evening in her office.

His hand came up to her jaw, taking it gently with his fingers and turning her toward him so he could look into her eyes. "I don't know why, when I picked a woman to marry and have children with, I couldn't have found someone more like you."

Samantha froze for a second, then muttered, "You don't even know me."

"I'm a little smarter than I used to be. I know that you're kind and generous and that you go to incredible lengths to make little children smile. And somehow I know you'd never hurt my children the way Elena did."

"Joe?" she said, in a panic now, because he was coming closer, his gaze intent on her mouth. He was going to kiss her, and she simply couldn't let him.

"It's scary, isn't it?" he asked.

"Scary?"

He nodded, so close she could almost taste him. "Because I'm very attracted to you."

Samantha backed away as far as she could, until the cushions were flat against her back, but still he was coming closer, coming to kiss her. Samantha took both her hands and shoved Joe, who'd twisted around to face her, until he fell to the floor.

From his spot on the floor Joe looked up at her and tried to figure out how he could have so totally misread the situation. Baffled, he stayed where he was and watched her squirm.

"I'm sorry," she said. "Are you hurt?"

"Doc, I've been thrown from a bull before. You're not going to hurt me by shoving me off my own sofa."

Color flooded her cheeks, and he cursed the fact that he found her so damned attractive.

Women, he thought. He'd never understand them.

He should have quit trying, should have left them alone, should definitely have left *her* alone.

"I'm sorry," she said again, and he simply couldn't leave things this way.

"All you had to do was say no. I'm not the kind of man who forces himself on a woman."

"I know."

"You do?"

She nodded, swallowed hard and looked everywhere but at him. Joe just didn't get it. She liked him. He knew it. And he liked her. She was pretty, in this soft feminine sort of way. And kind and sweet. She loved kids and tasted like heaven to kiss. What more could he want in a woman, even if he wasn't supposed to want any woman?

"I think I should go," she said, standing up.

Joe held out a hand to her, and she helped him to his feet, then pulled her hand away.

"I'm sorry Luke was so upset today. I...I didn't know what to say to him, and nothing short of a promise to bring his mother back would have satisfied him. I knew I couldn't promise that, so..."

"It's all right," he insisted. "I'll take care of Luke."

She nodded. "I'd better go."

Joe walked her to the door. When she had it open, he put his hand on her arm, holding her there beside him when she would have left. "Just tell me one thing, okay?"

She looked down at his hand on her arm, not at him. "If I can."

"What's wrong?"

Samantha shrugged. "I don't know what you mean."

"We were eating each other up in your office this evening," he insisted.

"No, I—"

"Don't even try to tell me you didn't like that kiss. I know better."

Her face turned toward the door, she said, "You're not making this very easy."

"It's not easy for me, either, and then, in another way, it's far too easy," he said gently, because he knew it was easy to spook her. "But I don't know about you. Tell me why it's so scary for you."

"You have kids," she said haltingly.

"Yes. What do the kids have to do with this?"

"I can't...I made a promise to myself. I'm not going to get involved with any man who has kids."

"Why?"

"Because it complicates things..."

"Yes," he said. It did complicate things. He'd met women who had absolutely no interest in having kids or being around them. Hell, he'd been married to one, except she hadn't figured that out until after they already had two kids. But Samantha Carter loved kids. There was absolutely no question in his mind about that. So her explanation made absolutely no sense. Why would she even try to tell him that? She had to know he wouldn't believe it.

"Doc, you love kids."

She nodded. "But I'm around them all day."

"So? You're telling me you get tired of them? That all you want of kids is what you get in the office?"

"No," she admitted.

"Have you ever been married?" He started firing off the questions.

"Yes."

Something inside his gut clenched tight before he could get the next question out. "Divorced?"

"Yes."

Thank goodness. "No kids?"

"No." She took it like a punch in the stomach. "I don't have any children."

"Why not?"

"Joe?" She was near tears again, and she looked sad, vulnerable.

Damn, he thought. Who'd hurt her so badly?

He pulled her into his arms again. She came without any form of protest and he held her, doing his best to comfort her and not to let any sexual thing enter into it, which was hard. But he could do it. Because he was worried about her and he didn't want to scare her off.

"Just tell me," he said. "I've told you the worst thing that ever happened to me. Tell me the worst for you."

"It hurts," she said.

"I know," he said tenderly, taking her face in his hands and kissing the tip of her nose. "Everybody gets hurt, Doc. Everybody. Who hurt you? Your ex?"

She nodded, her lashes flickering down, and Joe noticed they were dark and spiked together with the moisture from her tears. He kissed that away, as well, wishing he could kiss away the hurt just as easily.

Something was happening here, something that scared him because it was so powerful. But something that felt deliciously right, as well. He hadn't wanted another woman in the time since his wife left. He'd been so busy trying to keep his head above water with the kids and his job and the house that he hadn't had time to even think about another woman.

But Samantha...she was so soft and so pretty, so vulnerable, so nice. She had the most beautiful smile, and she worked hard to make little children smile, as well.

And she needed him. He was old-fashioned enough to feel a little kick in the gut at the idea of a woman truly needing him, of being able to take care of all her needs, fix all the things that hurt her and made her sad.

"Let me in, Doc. Let me help," he said. "Tell me

about Abbie. She's a little girl, and she's upset. Why's she upset?''

''She misses me.''

''Why does she miss you? Why can't you see her?''

''Because her father doesn't love me anymore. He's in love with someone else now, which means I not only lost him, I lost his daughters. My daughters, I thought. I loved them more than he did. I spent more time with them than he did, more time with them than I did with him, actually. Which may be one of the reasons he found someone else. He's never been that into his kids' lives, and I suppose he couldn't understand why I would be, either. He's much happier when he's the center of attention, and I guess he is now. With his new wife. And I'm here all alone. I'm kicking myself for being so blind to fall for him, and even worse, for falling for his daughters.''

''Oh, Samantha,'' he said.

''I loved them. I loved them very much. Their mother died when they were just babies, so they'd never really had a mother, and they needed me so much. And I loved them, Joe. And I miss them, and they miss me.''

''And he won't let you see them anymore?''

''I did at first, but he got married again right away, and I guess things weren't going so smoothly between his new wife and the girls, and he blamed me for that. The girls wanted to be with me, and as long as they could be, they weren't giving her a chance. So after a while he asked me not to see them anymore. He doesn't even want me to talk to them. Richard's decided they have to get on with their lives with him and his new wife.''

''I'm sorry,'' Joe said. ''He's an idiot.''

"I know. But I still miss the girls."

She was near tears again. Joe held her and tried to comfort her, all the while wishing he could wring a certain man's neck.

"I'm sorry," he repeated when she finally pulled away from him.

"How long has it been?" he said.

"Almost a year. I finally decided I just had to start over somewhere else. It was too hard to be in Seattle just a few miles away from them. Too tempting to call them or drive by their house or the park where they liked to play. My father left me some money, and a former colleague of his was having health problems. I agreed to cover for him for a few months and try out the practice here to see if I might want to buy it from him."

"So...do you like it here?"

"It's a nice town," she said. "I haven't done much but work, but I like the practice. The kids are great. The office staff's fabulous."

"You're just lonely?"

She nodded.

"Me, too," he said. "Seems like there ought to be something we could do about that, Doc."

"Joe, I told you...the kids? You have great kids, and you seem like a very nice man, but the idea of getting involved with any man who has children, children I could lose again... I can't do that. It scares me to death."

"I know. I've spent the past year watching my kids get their hearts broken by a woman I once loved. A woman I trusted. I made a lousy choice when I picked a mother for my kids, and now my kids are paying for it. So you're not the only one who's gun-shy—with good reason."

"Which means we're absolutely wrong for each other," she said.

She stepped away from him and picked up her purse. Like, she was going to just walk out of his life? And that was going to be the end of it? She went to open the door. Hell, she was going to leave. He hated that idea.

"I don't think so," Joe said, pushing the door shut.

She turned around to face him. "But you said you didn't want to get involved with anyone, either. It's too big a risk."

"Is it?" he said.

"Yes."

"Samantha, I don't want to hurt you. And the last thing I intend to allow is for my kids to be hurt again."

"Then we can't do this. It's all wrong. I already love Luke a little bit, and Dani…she's adorable. It would be too easy to fall for them."

Joe swore. "They need someone right now. It would be really easy for them to fall for any woman who paid them a little attention, especially someone as kind and caring as you are," he admitted, thinking if this was what it was like to be a grown-up, he didn't like it at all. If it meant having to be smart and careful and think a whole lot about everything before he did it, he didn't like it one bit.

"So we can't do this," she said. "We just can't."

Joe frowned, thinking he had her close enough to touch. Close enough to grab and haul into his arms and kiss senseless. Until this whole thing between them didn't seem like a bad idea at all.

He reached out and touched her hair, instead, stroking along the back of her head. She trembled a bit and leaned a little closer to him.

"I like you, Doc. I like you a lot."

"I like you, too," she whispered.

"Don't suppose you're the kind of girl who'd go for a nice, simple, steamy affair, would you? Something clandestine and purely carnal? Something that felt really good?"

She blushed and laughed, and thankfully she didn't seem insulted.

"Didn't think so," Joe said easily.

"I've never been any good at those no-strings kind of things."

He nodded. He knew it right away. "It's probably for the best. I think I could get all tangled up inside of you without even halfway trying. Still, being a grown-up about it is hell, isn't it?"

"Yes." She laughed again. Then she looked sad again. "I promised myself I was going to start over here. That I was going to be smart. New practice. New house. New friends…"

"New man?" he suggested.

"Maybe."

"A totally unattached man?"

"Yes."

"Well, that makes sense, Doc. That makes a lot of sense."

"I guess I should probably get to it," she said.

Joe nodded, his hands tightening on her shoulders. "Which means this is goodbye. You know, in Texas, a handshake just doesn't do it when it comes to goodbye, Doc."

"Oh?" she said, smiling shyly up at him. "How do people say goodbye in Texas?"

"A slap on the back sometimes. A bear hug between really good friends." He leaned down and nuzzled the tip of his nose against hers, their breaths mingling, as he thought about pinning her body against the wall with his and just not letting her go. "And when the other person smells really good, like you do, sometimes…"

She laughed. "Sometimes?"

"We do this…"

He settled his mouth over hers, and hers opened willingly, eagerly. Something about the taste of her went right to his head, making him dizzy and weak and needing to hang on to her to keep standing. He pulled her body to his, nearly pulling her off her feet, and groaned as she settled against him.

It was a long, slow, utterly delicious kiss, and he never wanted it to end. His body was hard and hurting, his brain going foggy and forgetting why this was all wrong.

She was different, he told himself. She was so different from Elena.

But how did he know that? He'd only known her for a little more than a day. How could he take that chance? Luke already thought she was pure magic, and Joe thought the same thing himself.

What if she'd cast a spell over both of them, and they just couldn't see straight anymore? Joe was half-serious about that part. He couldn't think about anything but her, getting closer to her, getting all these clothes from between them and getting skin to skin, right now.

He could have her here against the wall, and to hell with all the reasons he shouldn't.

He shuddered, pushing her back against the wall and pinning her there with his body. His hard throbbing body.

Finally he broke off the kiss. Her eyes slid open, and she looked dazed and every bit as confused as he felt. He touched her reverently, softly, getting off on the sight of his big tanned hand against the pale skin along her collarbone, coming tantalizingly close to her breasts.

"You're somethin' else, Doc."

He kissed her one more time, deeply, and then backed away completely, breathing hard and unable to take his eyes off her. She looked up at him, like he might come at her again and take her so hard and so fast it would make her head spin. He could do it, he realized. He could forget all the reasons he shouldn't and just do it. But it would be wrong, absolutely wrong.

"Sorry. I got a little carried away," he said.

"Me, too," she admitted, which he thought was generous of her.

Still breathing hard, he said, "Samantha, we've got to talk about this. Maybe there's a way to do this…a way to play it safe and make sure nobody gets hurt."

"No," she said. "You were right. It's too risky."

"But—"

"I just couldn't take it, Joe. I couldn't take losing one more thing I'd come to love, or one more person. I couldn't stand it."

"Okay," he said, backing off completely. He had no arguments against something like that.

"I really have to go," she said.

He nodded, seeing the tears in her eyes, tears that would likely fall the minute she got out his door. Dammit, he thought. He'd made her cry.

Chapter Five

The light on her answering machine was blinking when Samantha got back to the house she'd leased. Wearily she sat down on the stool and hit the button that made the messages play.

Richard's voice came to her, telling her quite coldly that he understood his daughter had called her that afternoon and that he would appreciate it if she did her best to discourage such contact. It was time, after all, that they all moved on with their lives.

Sam didn't know whether to cry some more or throw the phone across the room. But she wasn't a violent person, nor one given to fits of temper, and she was so tired, so hurt. She curled up into a ball in the middle of her lonely bed and gave herself permission to feel sorry for herself—at least until morning.

She'd do something tomorrow to make things better. To help her get on with her life—help her build a

life without Richard or the girls, without Joe Morgan
and his sad lonely kids, either. Without soft sweet
kisses that took her breath away, and laughter that for
the moment had made her remember there were some
good things left in the world. She could do that, she
told herself as she lay there in her misery. She could
make a life for herself here. She could be happy again.
She just had to get up and do something to make herself happy, and she would. Tomorrow.

It was harder than Samantha thought it would be.
She tossed and turned all night. Despite her resolve to
put all this behind her, she alternated between feeling
bad about the girls and daydreaming about the Morgans.

Groggy from lack of sleep after two nights of this,
she climbed into the shower and started humming a
song about cowboys, about women who shouldn't let
their babies grow up to be cowboys. She didn't understand why not. Her cowboy seemed quite nice.

Still sleepy, she rinsed her hair and shut off the
shower. It was Saturday, and she refused to work
weekends because she thought every kid who had to
go to the dentist at least deserved a few hours off from
school. It was the only bright spot many of them saw
in a trip to the dentist.

Still, it made for a long empty day for her, another
to follow on Sunday.

Samantha dried off, wrapped her hair in a towel, her
body in another, then padded out of the bathroom. She
had to have a cup of coffee—now, before she did one
more thing. She headed for the kitchen with her arms
over her head and not quite able to see, because the
towel on her head was slipping.

And found herself face-to-face with a toddler, a red-headed toddler with freckles and a button nose, eating a doughnut and walking down the hall in her rented house.

She screamed, couldn't help it. And then the kid screamed, too, and started to cry for his mommy. The doughnut, forgotten in his haste, lay crumbling on the carpet while Samantha clutched her towel.

She didn't want to be naked in front of an unknown toddler.

And when she looked up again, she decided the toddler must have found his dad, because he was hanging on to some man for dear life and pointing to her and babbling things Samantha couldn't understand.

She stood there speechless, clutching her towel, when June, the real-estate agent who'd rented her the house, came around the corner with a woman she bet was the hysterical toddler's mother.

"Oh, Samantha. You're home?"

"Yes," Samantha said.

"We knocked," June assured her, then turned to the man and his little boy, who was finally calming down. "Mr. Blake, this is the tenant I mentioned to you. Why don't you and your wife wait for me in the kitchen? I'll be right there."

The man grinned at Samantha, then turned and left with the little boy, and still Samantha just stood there, mortified.

"I'm sorry," June said. "I had no idea you were here, and I normally wouldn't show the house without notifying you first, but we were looking at a house down the street this morning and when we drove by this house, the Blakes wanted to see it, as well."

"Oh," Samantha said. Normally she would have

rented an apartment, but the rental market was tight, and unless she was willing to put up with institutional furnishings at a corporate apartment-type place, they all wanted a year's lease. This was close to her office. It had been empty for months after the owner moved out, and he'd been willing to lease it month to month, provided she made a hefty deposit. Which she thought would allow her to try out the community, but still move on if she wanted to.

"I guess I should tell you," June said. "The owner dropped the price last week. I think we'll be showing the house more often now."

"Oh." Great, Samantha thought. She could have a whole parade of toddlers and their fathers catching her in her towel.

"But we'll call next time. Promise."

Samantha did not feel the least bit reassured. "You're going to sell this house out from under me, aren't you."

"Well...maybe." June smiled, then remembered who she was talking to. "But I'll help you find something else. You said you might want to buy something of your own once you had time to get to know the community."

"But I have a lease," Samantha said.

"Month to month. That's what you wanted, but it works both ways. The owner can also terminate the arrangement if the house sells. Sorry." June hesitated, but just for a moment. "Uhh...since we're here already, you don't mind if I show the Blakes the rest of the house, do you?"

"I'll just get dressed first," Samantha said.

"Of course." Ever the salesman, June added, "And

I could come by this afternoon and show you some new places. We'll find just the thing for you.''

Joe sent Dani to her grandparents, and he and Luke had the house to themselves. He couldn't stall any longer. He had to talk with Luke now.

"Look, Dad!" Excited, Luke wiggled one of his bottom teeth back and forth with his tongue. "Cool, huh? It'll be out by morning, I bet."

Great, Joe thought. One more tooth down. Ninety-three to go, unless Joe put a stop to this. Of course, putting a stop to this pretty much meant breaking his kid's heart—the last thing Joe wanted to do. But he couldn't let this go on.

"Luke, you and I have to talk,''. he said as he and his son stood in the kitchen contemplating the empty cabinets that Joe hadn't yet filled this weekend with groceries.

His stomach growling, Luke looked worried. "Did I do somethin' wrong?"

"No." Joe picked up the cereal box and ignored the little voice in his head that said children could not live by cereal alone. Luke did, and he was growing like a weed. "Frosted? Or honey-coated?"

Luke considered quite seriously before announcing, "Both. Is this about Cynthia Webber's hair?"

Joe winced as he filled the plastic bowl. "What about Cynthia Webber's hair?"

"'Cause I didn't do it. Honest."

"Get the milk, Luke." Joe took the bowl of cereal to the table, then made a bowl for himself. If seven-year-olds could live off sugar-coated cereal, so could he.

Luke brought the milk and Joe poured. Luke dug

into his like a pig at a trough. With milk dribbling down his chin, he said, "I never cut her hair off. Honest."

Joe groaned, then practically roared, "Then who did?"

"I dunno."

"Luke!"

"'Kay, I know. But I didn't do it. Do I have to rat on Ritchie, 'cause he's my friend."

"He cut off her hair? At school?"

Luke grinned. "It was so cool. She screamed and screamed. And then she started to cry. And Miss Reynolds turned all red in the face."

"Luke, I don't want to get called to school again because you've been misbehaving. Understood?"

His excitement fading, the worried look back, Luke said, "Yes, Dad."

And then Joe felt like a heel. "Hey, buddy?"

"Hmm?"

"I love you."

"I love you, too, Dad."

"How 'bout we go to the park later? Maybe we can find a little pickup game of football?"

"'Kay."

"But you've got to listen to me about something first, okay?"

Luke nodded.

"It's about the teeth. And your mother. Luke?"

"Yeah." He kicked one of his shoes against the other and looked like he was getting ready to take a punch in the gut.

Damn.

Joe forced himself to go on. "Sometimes grown-ups do things that just don't make sense, Luke. Things we don't understand. I'm sorry your mother's gone. I know you miss her, and if I could bring her back to you, I would. But I can't.''

"You could make her come back," Luke insisted.

Joe wished he could sink right into the floor, rather than face his son's request. He had to face the possibility that it might be best if Luke never saw his mother again, that all she would ever do was hurt him and disappoint him. And Joe didn't want her back under those circumstances.

But for Luke? What did he want for Luke? He couldn't tell his kid that his mother was a rotten person. Or that she was acting like one.

"Luke, remember when we talked about following the rules? About how, when you're a kid, you have to do what your parents say, because they know things you just don't know and they're trying to take care of you and keep you safe?''

Luke nodded solemnly.

"I'm not your mother's parent. I can't tell her she has to come back here, and even if I did, she doesn't have to do what I tell her. Because she's a grown-up. When you get to be a grown-up, you get to make decisions for yourself, and your mother decided to go away.''

It was a terrible thing to say to a kid. But Joe had found out the hard way that there were no pretty lies to explain this away. Elena was gone, and there were only so many excuses he could make. God knows, he'd made them all already.

She took a trip. She got sick. She had to help a friend. She was coming back soon. The list was endless, and the kids hadn't bought any of it. The more excuses he made, the more his kids believed he was lying to them, and he was all they had left. He had to be straight with them.

"Why did she go away?" Luke asked tearfully.

"I don't know. She didn't tell me."

"Do you think she still loves us?"

Ouch. That hurt. Honesty, Joe reminded himself. What could he honestly say?

"Luke, I can't imagine anyone not loving you and Dani."

"I don't like Dani sometimes," he said.

"Well, she's your sister. I think you're allowed to not like her sometimes. But you still love her."

Luke shrugged. "I guess so."

"Samantha said you were mad at her."

"She can bring my mom back."

"No, Luke. She can't."

"She's magic."

"She pulls quarters from behind little boys' ears. Moms aren't quarters."

"Samantha's magic. I know it. She's the tooth fairy. I know 'cause she looks just like the one in the book, and the book is magic. And so is she."

"Remember what we said about grown-ups? They make their own decisions. Your mother decided to go. And until she decides she wants to come back, nothing can bring her back. Not magic. Or wishes. Or the teeth you've been putting in that jelly jar in your closet."

"She told you," Luke said accusingly.

"Yes, Samantha did. Because you can't go around school pulling other kids' teeth. We talked about this, Luke. If a bunch of teeth would bring your mother back, I'd take you into the garage, give you some pliers and let you pull every tooth I have."

"Do you have any that are loose?"

"No." Joe put his head in his hands and took a big breath, because this wasn't going at all the way he'd hoped.

"It would hurt a lot to pull 'em if they're not even loose," Luke said, all seriousness now.

"Buddy, I would do it for you if it would work. I'd do anything. But it won't work. Do you understand what I'm saying? Do you believe me about the teeth and the wishes?" Luke kept squirming, so Joe had to work hard to look him in the eye, to make sure Luke heard and understood. "Luke? A bunch of teeth aren't going to bring your mother back."

"'Kay." Luke hung his head, tears running down his cheeks. "Is she ever coming back?"

"I don't know, Luke. Honest to God, I just don't know." Joe pulled Luke to his side and held on tight. "But I know one thing."

"What?" Luke mumbled miserably.

"I'm here. And I'm not going anywhere." Joe almost choked on the words himself. "Believe me?"

Luke nodded and buried his head against his father's side.

Samantha worked constantly the next week, trying to make herself so tired she didn't have time to think or be tempted to pick up the phone and call Seattle or be disappointed when she saw nothing more of Joe or Luke. She was moving on, after all, and moving for real, it seemed.

The previous Sunday her real-estate agent gave her official notice that the house in which she was living had been sold and that Samantha had to find another place to live.

"We'll find you something perfect," June said,

strolling into the living room with an armful of note-books and making herself comfortable by spreading her things across the coffee table. "Just tell me what you want, and I'll find it."

Daughters, Samantha thought, thinking of the ones she lost. She wanted daughters. And then she found that image sharing space inside her head with Luke Morgan's impish face, with the feel of Joe's arms wrapped around her, the sound of his voice whispering in her ear. Too bad, Samantha told herself. June didn't have any of those things in her house books. Samantha couldn't take out a mortgage and buy them, either.

But she could find herself a house. She could take that one step toward what she wanted. If she was going to build a life here, she had to have a place to live, and there was no need to wait to find a man to provide one for her. She had money of her own and a good job. She was a modern woman. She could find her own house—an absolutely perfect house. And when she found a man to marry, a man she trusted to have children with, they could all live there.

It was a very positive step. An optimistic one. Surely she could take one positive step toward the life she wanted to have. She wouldn't get anywhere sitting here feeling sorry for herself and waiting for the world to somehow bring all the things she wanted to her.

She and June spent twenty minutes flipping through photographs and home descriptions, looking over the maps of the community and finally heading out to look at three places that were close by.

One was too big. One was too small. One seemed just right—the size, the neighborhood, the price, the style, and yet Samantha knew it just wasn't her house. As June drove her back home late that afternoon, Sa-

mantha turned her head toward the side window while
June rattled on about depreciation and interest rates
and tax advantages.

Gazing sadly at the passing scenery and trying not
to listen to anything June said, Samantha caught sight
of a For Sale sign in a yard overgrown with weeds.
Curious, she thought, because all the other houses on
the street had beautifully maintained yards, with little
rock borders and flower beds and vines and bulbs. It
was a charming neighborhood, a place full of real
homes.

"What's this place?" Samantha said.

Ready to latch on to the least show of interest, June
jerked the car to the curb and pulled out her handy-
dandy house book. "What's the address?"

Samantha looked to the end of the street, then to
the numbers on the porch column. "Three-ten Dogwood Lane."

She'd had dogwoods in her backyard when she
was growing up. Scrawny ugly trees that seemed to
have no substance at all, no backbone. But in the
spring…Samantha smiled. She could see them filled
with the brightest bursts of pinks and spring whites,
delicate little blossoms that absolutely transformed
those trees into something magical for a few short
weeks.

June started reading the listing information to her.
"Seventy-five years old."

Seventy-five? She'd need a live-in handyman.

"Five bedrooms, four baths."

An army could sleep there.

"Full basement."

Which would leak for sure.

"A one-acre lot."

She'd need a tractor to mow it.

"It's all wrong for me," Samantha said, gazing at the house. The real trouble was, it reminded her of her own home, the one where she'd grown up.

It had all sorts of interesting angles to it, a wide shaded front porch, so many windows she'd pay a fortune to cover them and another fortune to heat the house.

June named a price, then added, "That can't be right. It's much too small a figure for this much space. Let me see..."

Samantha watched as June finally looked up and saw the house.

"God, it's a mess."

"No, it's not." Samantha felt she had to defend it for some reason.

"Well," June backpedaled, "it's a steal for this price. And the neighborhood... You know what people say about buying a house—location, location, location. You can fix anything about a house except its location."

True, Samantha thought. But this house needed a tremendous amount of fixing. Still, they could just look. What was the harm in looking? "Can we go inside? Now?"

June peered through the trees toward the front porch. "If there's a lockbox, we can look."

They climbed out of the car and walked to the front door. Beneath her feet, the boards that formed the front porch creaked and sagged ominously. The white paint was flaking, giving the house a dingy and rather sad appearance. Still, Samantha was excited.

June extracted the key from the lockbox, and they let themselves in. Dust scattered as the wind rushed in. Samantha watched as sunlight streamed through the windows and the dust floated back down to the floor, which was hardwood. Obviously it had been mistreated over the years, but it was real hardwood.

She could sand it, polish it, make it shine.

There was a huge fireplace in the corner, an elaborately carved wooden mantel, equally in need of attention. But it could be magnificent. She just knew it.

In the back she saw a yard filled with trees, the ground covered by a blanket of leaves that no one had bothered to rake. The lot was wide, heavily treed, ending in what she suspected was a stream that ran across the back of the property. It was a children's paradise, she decided. Lots of trees, grass, a stream—they could play for hours. She had, in a place just like this.

Why the thought didn't make her sad, when she had no children to play here, she simply didn't understand. But she felt excited seeing a mismatched collection of boards hammered together high in the tree to form a tree house, a swing hung from one of the branches, the faint outline of a ball field laid out in the grass.

The kitchen was ancient, with linoleum right out of the fifties, minimal counter space, hardly any cabinet space. No dishwasher. It was like their kitchen at home, but it was a big room. She could do anything she wanted here, with time and money at her disposal.

There was a huge family room that opened to the right off the kitchen. Just a big room, with lime-green carpet, but it had a wonderful view of the yard and the dogwood trees she liked so much.

Passing through the formal dining room, she found herself at the front of the house again, facing the staircase, which curved gracefully to the right and immediately had Samantha thinking of children sliding down it just for fun.

No kids, she reminded herself. She had no kids. But still, she was already thinking of paint choices and window coverings. It was insane.

Upstairs she saw big bedrooms, but they had no closet space and tiny bathrooms. But she was no slave to fashion, and she never spent that much time in the bathroom, anyway. How much space did she need?

Walking downstairs again, she thought of the sadly neglected woodwork, the peeling paint, the draftiness of the place, the sheer size of it. She hadn't even seen the basement yet.

June clattered along behind her in her high heels with her clipboard in hand as she scribbled down notes. "We'll need to hire an inspector to go over every inch, of course."

If she was going to buy this house.

Samantha stepped into the kitchen, where someone had left a bar stool, and sat down. There was enough dust in the place that she could have written her name in the film covering the stained and chipped counter. The floor here dipped and swayed, and the wallpaper was falling down in spots.

How could she possibly want this house?

June was chattering on about escrow accounts and counteroffers and financing options, then got on her cellular phone to see what she could find out about the place. When she was done, she found Samantha in the kitchen. "It's not bad," she said. "The owner was an elderly widow who didn't have any family nearby to help her and didn't trust anyone to do odd jobs for her. So she really let the place go. And the relatives haven't been willing to put any money into it to fix it up. They're determined to sell it as is. If we're lucky, you may just be looking at mostly cosmetic work here. Of course, we could—''

Samantha cut her off. ''Could you give me a minute alone here? Please?''

''Of course.'' June took her paraphernalia and headed for the door. ''Take all the time you need. I'll wait in the car.''

Samantha sat there. Closing her eyes, she let herself hear the sounds of the house, the wind in the trees, the chirping of the birds, the muted sounds of the street.

It felt good to be here, she realized. It was peaceful, soothing and very, very familiar.

Being here made her think of her father, made her remember Sunday mornings when he'd donned his chef's apron and dirtied half the pots and pans in the house as he prepared one meal—Sunday brunch. It made her think of summer evenings in the backyard with him, because he was determined to make a baseball player of her. Strange, she could almost taste his blueberry pancakes, hear the crack of the bat when she finally blasted one home.

Turning around, she caught a whiff of something very familiar, something bitter with a hint of sweetness. His cigars. She could have sworn for a moment she smelled his cigars.

''Daddy?'' she said aloud in a terribly childish voice as she wrapped her arms around her middle.

She hadn't felt this close to him in the longest time, hadn't felt she needed him this much in years. Somehow she imagined she might reach out and touch him then, even if he had been dead for a year.

Samantha stayed there for a long time, soaking up

his presence, letting it chase away the awful loneliness inside her and absorb some of the pain.

Finally she stepped outside onto the concrete slab that was the terrace, felt sunshine streaming through the trees and falling against her face. It left her warm and strangely satisfied. The wind was light, carrying with it the scent of the trees and the fallen leaves.

And the house?

It was a mess, but she didn't care. The place seemed to comfort her in some way. She didn't understand how or why, but she'd take her comfort where she could find it.

She was going to buy this house, and maybe she could make a home here, make a life for herself.

Chapter Six

Joe waited until the third day Luke complained of a toothache before he took his son to see Samantha again. He thought he'd shown admirable restraint. He hadn't given in at the first pathetically fake protestation of pain from his son. No, he'd waited until Luke had perfected an Oscar-worthy performance, until there was that nagging sense of parental inadequacy that had Joe wondering if he was being a terrible father for ignoring what was, even if the most remote possibility, genuine pain on the part of his son. And then he went.

After a week of moping around the house, Joe, his son and his daughter all went to the dentist's office. You'd have thought he'd bought circus tickets the way they all reacted.

They'd all fussed over their appearance. He was no better than his kids. He slicked back Dani's hair into a reasonable facsimile of a braid and let her wear her hot-pink sneakers with the laces that were three times too wide and had pink hearts on them. She peeled off her plaid school smock and underneath had on a plain white shirt but her most fashionable blue-jean shorts, the ones with purple beads embroidered into the fabric to form little purple flowers. And she'd stored some of her favorite jewelry in her school backpack—a series of plastic necklaces which she draped around her neck and somehow attached to her hair. He'd never understood the hair-necklace bit, but she liked it, and for the first time all week she was happy. He let it go and took a miniature Madonna and a smiling Luke into Samantha's office.

He had merely had as much of a bath as he could in the sink at the construction site and changed his shirt. Luke showed no signs of holding the side of his mouth and moaning this morning, but they already had the appointment. They were going. They'd all see Samantha again.

Joe caught sight of her before she spotted them, so he saw every bit of her reaction to them. She looked tired, he thought, and maybe a bit sad. Then she saw Luke and Dani and positively beamed. She fussed over Dani's hair and drew a tongue depressor from her voluminous white coat that turned into a bouquet of flowers, which she presented to Dani.

But when she turned to Joe, she seemed to physically pull herself away, all without moving an inch. So, he thought, it was as hard for her as it was for him. Somehow that made things a little better and a whole lot worse.

"What seems to be the trouble now?" she asked,

obviously working hard to put a smile on her pretty face.

"Luke has a toothache," Joe said.

"Really?" she looked from Luke to Joe again.

Behind Luke's back, out of Luke's sight, Joe shook his head.

"Well, we'll just have to see about that," Samantha said, taking him by the hand and leading him into the stars room. "I have some medicine that I bet will fix you right up."

"Medicine?" Luke said, making a face, maybe seeing some flaws in his plan for the first time.

"Yes. It's great. There's just one little problem."

"What?" Luke asked cautiously.

"Where does the tooth hurt?"

Luke opened his mouth and stuck his own finger inside, then mumbled, "Here."

Samantha snapped on the light and shined it into Luke's mouth, then leaned down and peered inside. "Oh, no. That's what I was afraid of."

"What?" Luke sounded worried now.

"It's an unusual problem." Samantha nodded gravely. "I hardly ever see cases like this."

"Really?"

"Yes. I can fix it if it really hurts. But it would take a very special medicine I hardly ever use, and to get the special medicine all the way down to the spot that hurts…" She turned to the cabinet behind her and pulled out a very big-looking syringe with a long needle on it. "I'm afraid I'd have to use this."

Dani squeaked and wrapped herself around Joe's leg. Luke's eyes got as big as saucers and he looked horrified.

"My tooth doesn't hurt that much," he said quickly.

"Oh?" Samantha was remarkably serious-looking. "You're sure? Because I can fix it."

"Uh-huh. It's all better. See?" He opened up again and poked the end of his finger against the tooth. "It doesn't hurt a bit."

Samantha let him sweat for a minute. Bless her heart, she knew what Joe and his kids needed from her, and she gave it to them. "Well, if you're sure..."

"I am." Luke headed for the door. "Come on, Dad. It's better now."

"Do me a favor. Take your sister back to the waiting room so she can see the fairies," Joe said, then remembered the perils there. "And don't swipe anything this time."

"I won't," Luke said, looking thoroughly disgruntled now but taking his sister by the hand. "Come on, Dani. Let's go."

"I wanna see the tooth fairy," she said stubbornly as Luke pulled her down the hall.

"We will. You heard what Daddy said. I'm taking you to see them."

"No, the real one," Dani insisted.

"Come on." Luke dragged her along until they disappeared through the door that led to the waiting room.

Joe watched them go and then turned to face the woman who'd haunted his every waking moment for a week. She was every bit as beautiful as he remembered. Every bit as sweet and kind and genuine, and he suspected she'd taste just as sweet, as well. He couldn't get her out of his mind.

"Sorry about that," he said. "He's been complaining for three solid days, and I thought he was faking, but then I had to make sure. I kept worrying I'd go into his room one morning and find his mouth swollen up to three times its normal size and half his teeth falling out because I'd ignored something that was really wrong with him. All because I was so sure that all he wanted was to see you again.''

"It's all right. It's hard to know for sure sometimes.''

Joe nodded.

"Of course,'' she said, "now I've traumatized him with my big needle, and he may well not tell you if he ever has something truly wrong with his teeth because he's scared I'll give him a shot.''

"I'm sorry, Doc.''

"I work hard to keep the kids from being afraid of me,'' she said.

"I know, and I know it wasn't easy for you to do what you did. But that's what he needed. Otherwise, I'm afraid he'd have me trying to bring him back here every other day.''

"That's what I thought,'' she said. "He's still collecting teeth?''

"Not that I know of. I talked to him about his mother and wishes and magic and how lousy life can be sometimes, but I don't know if I convinced him of anything. I think he still believes you could bring his mother back.''

"Oh, Joe. I'm so sorry.''

"It's not your fault,'' he assured her.

"It is. Me and my silly costume. All these silly magic tricks.''

"No. It's not that at all. He's just dying to latch on to something to give him hope that his life's going to get back to normal someday. If it wasn't you, it would be something else.''

"I wish I could help him."

"So do I," Joe said sadly. "How 'bout you, Doc? How you doin'?"

"I'm okay," she claimed.

He reached out and touched her cheek, his thumb sliding lightly along the underside of her eye, which had a grayish tone. "Gettin' any sleep?"

She moved away, escaping even that light touch. "Not enough."

"I've been thinking about you," he confessed. "I haven't been sleeping that well myself."

"Joe," she protested, shaking her head. "I can't…"

"Okay," he said, stepping back. "If you're sure…"

"I am. I don't like it. But I am."

"You gonna be okay?"

She nodded. "I've decided to stay in town. I'm going ahead and buying this practice. And a house."

"Really?"

"Yes. I was renting a place month to month, and it sold right out from under me. I went out the next day with the real-estate agent and found something wonderful," she rushed on. "Well, not wonderful yet, but it will be. It's big and old and has a great backyard and big trees and…it reminded me of home. Mine, when I was a little girl. I felt at home there. So I bought it."

He frowned down at her, not wanting to think of Samantha making a home for herself and who she'd fill it with.

"It was a bit impulsive, I know," she explained. "But I can't keep drifting along like this."

"Of course," he said. He wanted her to be happy.

"It's over on Dogwood Lane, about ten minutes from here."

"The old Baldwin place?" he guessed.

She nodded.

"It needs a lot of work, Samantha."

"I know."

"You had it inspected?"

"Yes. All that stuff." She named an inspector he knew.

"Okay. He wouldn't have sugarcoated anything."

"He didn't. And I may have to take it slow, doing a little bit here and there, but that's okay. I have time. I just need to get a new roof before I move in and a few other necessities, and I'll be fine."

"You want me to come look at it? I'm booked up for the next few weeks, but I might be able to free up a crew to repair the roof."

"I don't think that would be a good idea."

"Okay," he said. "Just be careful who you hire."

"I will," she promised.

"If you want to call me and check 'em out..."

"Thanks," she said.

But he didn't think she'd call. He was afraid he'd never hear from her again, unless he stooped to faking a toothache himself. He wondered how long it would take before he'd consider that, just to see this sweet, skittish, magical woman one more time.

Something inside him was screaming not to let her go. Not to let this moment end. That there just had to be a way, even if he had as many reasons as she did to steer clear of any kind of involvement.

And the whole thing left him feeling even lousier than he had before. She'd given him hope, just for a little bit, that there might be a perfectly wonderful woman out there somewhere who'd be great not only for him but for his kids.

And maybe she was that woman, but they'd never know it, because she didn't want them.

Damn, Joe thought. What a lousy day.

Samantha frowned down at the list of contractors she'd gotten from the local builders' association, names she'd crossed off one by one. People were booked up. Spring had sprung, and everyone wanted to start working on their house right now. Some of the contractors couldn't even take time to come look at the job. Some of them kept her waiting for hours when she made an appointment for them to come. No way she was hiring them.

In the end she didn't have much choice.

There was Joe, whom she wouldn't let herself call, and a man named Abe Wilson.

She hadn't been that impressed with Abe. He drove the most battered-looking truck she'd ever seen, chain-smoked and no matter how hard she tried to make him stop, insisted on calling her "little lady." He also wasn't shy about telling her she should get herself a husband because he would understand all the things Abe was trying to explain to her about fixing up her old house. Still, Abe seemed to genuinely like the house and see its possibilities.

Samantha looked down at her list once again and at the calendar. She had to do something. Her deadline for getting out of the rental house was rushing ever closer.

She allowed herself one moment of longing for Joe—to call his number and have him fix her dream house for her. She could talk to him every day if she wanted. She could see him. But it would lead to nothing but trouble.

In the end that's what decided her.

Anybody but him, she told herself. She'd hire anybody but him.

Which was how she ended up with Abe.

She worked frantically over the next few weeks, so frantically she hardly had time to think about Joe and Luke and Dani. By day she juggled frantic phone calls from her contractor, her real-estate agent, mortgage companies, inspectors and insurance agents, trying to get everything done. And by night she packed and pored over paint chips and wallpaper samples, fabric swatches and cabinet styles, tile patterns and other endless details, right down to the shade of blue she'd like for the grout between the kitchen tiles.

It was crazy, but she did it, and she was too busy most of the time to be sad. The day she moved in, she was happier than she'd been in a long, long time. Since before her marriage to Richard fell apart, in fact. She felt that good.

Samantha brought only the things she absolutely had to have to live for the first few weeks, because the place was still a mess. Abe and his men seemed to have made the house more of a mess than it had been the first time she'd seen it, but she'd been warned that the construction process was a messy one.

She bedded down the first night in her own room at the top of the stairs and to the right, trying to get used to all the little unfamiliar sounds of the house settling around her, still finding it comforting just to be here.

She felt good here. Good things were going to happen for her here. She could feel it.

Drifting off to the faint sounds of thunder in the distance and the smell of rain coming in the window she'd opened, she slept deeply, dreamlessly, peacefully.

Until drops of water started dripping onto her forehead.

She came awake with a wet face, jerked out of bed and wiped the water off her cheek. There was a damp spot on the bed beside her pillow, and when she leaned over to see it, another drop of water fell on the back of her neck.

She yelped and jumped out of the way. Looking up, she saw water dripping from her ceiling.

"Oh, no!" she cried.

She became aware of the sound of rain pounding furiously on the roof. Her leaking roof!

Looking around the room, she saw leaks coming down from other spots all around the room.

Samantha ran downstairs, grabbing all the pots and pans she had, the pitchers, even the cups. She hurried upstairs and placed them all around the room and in the bedroom to her left, which was leaking, too, but they wouldn't do her much good for long.

Staring at the clock on the bedside table, she saw that it was shortly after midnight. On a Saturday night.

Who in the world could she call at this hour?

She tried Abe first. There was no answer. She got a machine at his office, a message that his cell phone was either turned off or out of range and no answer at his home. She let it ring and ring and ring.

Water was still dripping from her ceiling. It was still raining like crazy.

Samantha glanced out the window over the tops of the trees and thought about how few people she knew in this town. No one she could call at nearly one in the morning.

And then she thought of Joe. She wasn't that far from him. Only six blocks or so. She'd been so sad when she realized that he was so close and yet so far away, that he always would be. She'd missed him terribly these past two months.

And she shouldn't call him now. He was nothing to her.

She tried Abe one more time and got nothing. A drop of water hit her on the nose. She wanted to cry, but that would only make more water, the last thing she needed.

And then she called Joe.

He answered on the first ring, his voice as smooth and deep and sexy as ever.

"Hi," she said. "It's me." Which was a silly thing to say. She realized it right away. She always said the silliest things to him.

But if he saw anything silly about it, he didn't say. All he said was, "Samantha, what's wrong?"

"I'm so sorry for calling you so late…"

"Don't worry about it. I was up."

And then she had an awful thought—what if he wasn't alone? What if he was still awake at this hour, early on a Sunday morning, because he wasn't alone?

"Are you—" She stopped herself just in time. No way was she asking him that. "I'm sorry."

"Somehow I don't think you called for the reason I wanted."

"You wanted me to call you?"

"Yes," he said.

She closed her eyes, thinking she was so glad, so very glad. "Why did you want me to call?"

"Because you missed me. Because you were going crazy trying to forget me."

"I do miss you," she admitted. What was the point even trying to deny it?

"Thank goodness," he said.

"But that's not why I called. I called because my ceiling's dripping."

"Your ceiling?"

"No. I mean water. Water is dripping from my ceiling."

"Oh." Joe frowned and shook his head. Until that moment he hadn't been quite sure that he was awake and this was real. Because as fantasies went, this was a pretty good one. Samantha, all breathless and needy-sounding, finally calling him and telling him she missed him.

But it was raining like crazy tonight—he'd figured that out now. He was sprawled across his couch in a position that had left a crook in his neck, and the TV was still going, showing him a ball game from the West Coast. His big Saturday night—asleep in front of the TV and thinking about Samantha.

Who'd called him because Abe Wilson had botched the job on her roof. He knew she was in trouble the minute he'd heard she'd hired Abe. She had to have been desperate to hire Abe, and even more desperate now to call Joe. It had taken water coming from her ceiling, after all.

"How bad is it?" he asked.

"Bad. It's coming in in a dozen places. I've used

every pot and pan I have, and they're going to over-flow soon, and I don't know what else to do. I'm sorry. I tried to call my contractor—''

"Don't bother. It's Saturday night. Abe's drunk."

"He gets drunk every Saturday night?"

"He gets drunk most every night, Samantha. What were you thinking, hiring him? You were asking for trouble."

"I was thinking I had to get out of the house I rented, and I wanted to be in here, in this house right away, and nobody but him could start right away."

"Sam," he groaned.

"I was just going to let him do the roof. That was all. And then I was going to hire someone better. Really."

"Anybody but me," he said.

"Yes," she said miserably. "Anybody but you."

He picked himself up off the couch and started looking for his shoes, hoping she'd been as lonely without him as he'd been without her.

He didn't sound that upset, Samantha decided, throwing on some dry clothes so she could go to Joe's house.

He had kids there asleep, after all. He couldn't just rush off to her rescue and leave them. So she was going there. He'd insisted. She could stay there with the kids, and he would go do what he could to keep the rain from ruining her house tonight. If he was will-ing to come rescue her on a night like this, it was the least she could do. Sit in his warm dry house while his kids slept in their beds.

She wouldn't have to see them. They wouldn't even know she was there, and she could pretend *they* weren't there. No problem. Joe would do what he could for her poor roof, and she'd leave. No big deal.

She got to his house in ten minutes flat. He opened the door before she could even knock, and she fought the insane urge to throw herself into his welcoming arms. He looked every bit as tall and strong and good as she'd imagined in the past few endless weeks.

"Hi," she said shyly, standing in the foyer with water dripping off her and looking at him in his faded jeans and San Antonio Rodeo T-shirt.

He pulled the door closed behind her and said, "You're soaked. Let me get you a towel."

He did. She took it gratefully and wiped the moisture from her face and the worst of it from her hair and then stood there, not much but the towel between them. She held it like a shield, thinking she had to keep something right there between them.

"I just moved in today, and I couldn't even find my raincoat," she said. "I just got dressed and ran over here."

"It's all right. And there's no reason for you to stay in those wet things."

"Oh, I'm fine," she said.

But he didn't listen. He went to the laundry room and came back with a T-shirt and a pair of gym shorts, still warm from the dryer. They smelled like him. She took the clothes but made no promises about putting them on.

"Thank you for doing this."

"No problem," he said.

"I didn't know who else to call."

"It's all right, Samantha. The kids have been asleep for hours. I don't think they'll need anything, but I really couldn't leave them here by themselves."

"Of course not."

"Make yourself at home," he said. "I'll do what I can."

"Thanks."

And then she stood in the doorway and watched him head out into the rain, stood there thinking about how many times she'd watched Richard walk away from her and the girls, how seldom she'd wondered where he was going and who he might be with. How foolish she'd been. How much it had hurt in the end, when the truth came out. That he didn't love her anymore, that he didn't need her. That he could break her heart and walk away without a backward glance.

She had to be smart, she told herself. She had to be smart so she didn't get hurt again.

Samantha must have dozed on the couch, and she thought she was dreaming at first that she heard Abbie calling for her father. But then she woke up and realized it wasn't a dream. She wasn't back in Seattle, and the child wasn't Abbie. She was in Virginia at Joe's house, and the child crying out for her father was Dani.

Samantha got to her feet and ran down the hallway, following the urgent little voice, and found Dani sitting in the middle of her bed, the covers pulled up all around her like a shield, her eyes so big and the sound of thunder booming through her little-girl-pink bedroom.

Lightning lit the room for an instant. Dani shrieked again, and then Samantha heard more footsteps behind her a second before Luke burst into the room.

For a moment the three of them just looked at one

another, puzzled, scared, sleepy, uncertain what to do next, and then they all started talking at once.

"Daddy's not here," Luke said.

"An' there's thunder," Dani complained.

"It's all right," Samantha said, then did her best to explain about her roof and Joe going to fix it and that there was nothing to fear from the storm.

The children accepted it all with remarkable calm—until she tried to get them back to sleep. Dani wouldn't go with the storm scaring her, and Luke didn't say anything, but Samantha thought he was thinking the same thing.

"When it's really loud like this, Daddy lets us sleep in his bed," Dani said.

"Oh. Okay."

Off they went to Joe's bedroom, a no-nonsense room painted a faint chalklike color with a plain pine bed and a green comforter, green-striped sheets. This was not his ex-wife's doing. He'd redone this room after she left.

The children climbed into the bed and settled in. She hoped it would be okay with Joe when he came back.

"Well," she said, reaching for the bedside lamp. "Do you want this on or off?"

"On," Dani said.

"Off," Luke said.

They argued about that for a few minutes and finally agreed on a compromise—bedside lamp off, bathroom light on with the door open just a bit to bring dim light into the room.

Samantha leaned over them both, tucking them in tightly one by one, kissing them in turn.

Dani wrapped her arms around Samantha and

squeezed tight. Luke just lay there and looked sad and finally said, "You know exactly how to do it."

"What?"

"How to tuck us in."

Samantha thought he might as well have ripped her heart right out of her chest, wrung it out and shoved it back in. He knew exactly how to get to her.

She tried to shrug it off, as if it didn't mean anything at all. "I just thought that was the way it was done."

"I missed you," Luke said solemnly.

"Me, too," Dani said.

"You don't even know her," Luke insisted.

"Do, too. She gave me the glow-in-the-dark toofbwush, and she's my friend," Dani said. "We didn't think you was ever comin' back."

"Oh. I'm…I'm just here because I had some trouble at my house. Remember? I told you about it."

Dani nodded, looking like she didn't understand at all.

"You don't like us?" Luke said.

"Oh, of course, I do. I like you both. Very much."

"But you don't want to see us? You're too busy?"

"No. It's not that, Luke, not at all," she said. "You two need to get some sleep. Your father will be back anytime now."

"Where ya goin'?" Dani asked.

"Back to the living room," Samantha said.

"Uh-uh. You gotta stay here. It doesn't work if you don't stay here."

"What?"

"She'll still be scared, even if she's in Daddy's bed and even if I'm here. You gotta stay," Luke said.

"Oh."

Which was how she ended up putting on Joe's dry T-shirt and his gym shorts and climbing into Joe's bed, wedged between Joe's children. And sleeping better than she had in months.

Joe felt a bit like Papa Bear coming home to find three people snuggled up asleep in his bed. He was drenched and cold and tired, and despite all that, he stood there staring at them.

It was the last thing he'd pictured when he'd imagined Samantha in his bed, but there she was, looking for all the world like she belonged there. She was lying on her side facing Dani, who was wedged up against her spoon-fashion, Samantha's arm around her protectively. Luke was on his side, too, curled up against Samantha's back, and Joe found it hurt just to see them like this, all together, so trusting, seemingly so loving.

He wanted to climb right into that bed beside them, wanted all of them safe in arms.

She had none of Elena in her. He could swear that.

But then, he hadn't seen it in Elena at first, either. Hell, he hadn't even known what to look for, what was important to him back then. He and Elena had been having fun. That was all. And she was fine for having fun with, but she was for damned sure not the kind of woman to have children with.

He'd been so stupid, and his kids had been hurt so badly because of it.

He wouldn't do that to them again. He wouldn't put them at risk that way. Not until he was sure. And Samantha didn't want to put her heart on the line, either. He understood that. He didn't want to hurt her any more than he wanted his kids hurt.

So tomorrow she had to go. He'd hustle her out of here before the kids even woke up.

There, he thought, as he bent over and kissed the three of them good-night. He had everything figured out.

Chapter Seven

Samantha tried to roll over, but there was something wedged against her back keeping her from moving that way. She tried to go the other way, only to find that way blocked, as well.

She thought she heard water running and waited an instant to see if any was going to land on her again, but it didn't. So she cautiously opened her eyes to find sunlight streaming in the window and that the running water was coming from a shower.

She was in Joe's bed with Joe's kids beside her, and a moment later the water stopped and Joe stood in the bathroom door wearing nothing but a towel.

"Oh." She caught her breath.

He gave her a slow sexy smile and made a half-hearted effort to hold the towel in place. His hair was dark and still dripping, a cloud of steam billowing out of the bathroom around him and the fresh scent of him coming with it. She should have looked away, she knew, but she couldn't quite bring herself to.

He was beautiful.

Everywhere she looked. That broad chest sprinkled with little curling hairs that fanned out along his chest and narrowed to an intriguing line down his abdomen, disappearing into the dubious cover of the towel, which didn't quite meet at the ends. There was an eye-catching strip of nothing but skin along his right side and down one muscled thigh.

Oh, my.

Richard had been fifteen years older than she was, closer to her father's age than her own, and...well, maybe he'd once looked like this, but not at any time Samantha had known him. She wasn't sure she'd ever seen a man who looked as good as Joe did.

"Good morning," he whispered.

"Morning," she said, odd little flutters in her stomach making her voice sound breathless and strange.

Dani stirred beside her, turning over and shifting closer.

"The storm woke her," Samantha said, then looked down at her predicament, his kid, his bed. She'd spent the entire night here. "I didn't mean to fall asleep, but they said this is what you do when they wake up scared. They didn't want me to leave."

"That's what we do. Crowd into my bed."

"I didn't mean to stay," she said, coloring profusely now.

"It's not a problem, Doc. Sorry I woke you. I thought I'd grab a shower and clear out of here before I disturbed anyone, but I forgot to grab clean clothes before I walked in there."

"Oh. It's all right," she said, blushing the moment

the words left her mouth. It was certainly no hardship to see him this way.

"You know," he said with a grin, "if you slide out of that bed very carefully, they might sleep for another couple of hours. We could have some peace and quiet."

"Oh. Of course," she said, carefully disentangling herself from both children and climbing over his daughter.

He caught her by the arm when she was off balance and trying not to disturb Dani, and she tried very hard not to think of the fact that he was all but naked or of the way it felt to have his hands on her, just helping her out of his bed.

She tucked the covers around his sleeping children and tried not to think of the last time she'd slept this way. One night when Richard had been away on a business trip—or maybe off with his soon-to-be wife—and Abbie had crept into Samantha's bed, Sarah joining them that morning, the three of them lying there for a long time laughing and sharing stories and planning their day. She blinked back the memory, determined that her life would never be that way again.

Joe grabbed some clothes out of the closet and then pulled Samantha out into the hallway with him. She stood there trying not to draw in the scent of him or even think about kissing him or anything like that. Instead, she looked down at his rumpled shirt that she wore and pushed her hair back from her face and tried to ignore the implied intimacy of the situation. She shouldn't have stayed.

"It can't be that bad, Doc," he said, taking her chin in his hand and tilting her face up to his.

"It just...it's hard," she said. "It makes me remember..."

"Abbie?" he asked.

"Yes."

"And her sister? What's her name?"

"Sarah."

"Sorry. I don't want to bring up bad memories for you."

"It's not your fault. It's just...this is what my life was. Being here with someone else's children, acting like a mother when I wasn't, when I didn't have any of the rights a mother has. That's what's still messing with my head and my heart, and I look at you and those two kids and..."

"It's too soon. The worst possible time."

"Yes." Everything that scared her, everything she wanted to forget. "And for your kids, too. They're lonely, too. They need someone. It would be just as easy for them to get hurt as it would be for me."

"I know."

They'd latched on to her from the first moment, so eager, so lost.

"It's an impossible situation," she argued.

"I'm not disagreeing with you, Doc. I'm not trying to make this any harder than it already is."

"You're not?"

"No. Do you think I'm going to push you into doing something you don't want to do? No matter how I might want it, even if I know it's not smart at all?"

"I don't know what you're going to do. I just know that one of us needs to be smart and strong and careful, and I'm not sure I can be that person anymore, and you're... You're practically naked, Joe, and you're...just about perfect, too."

"Perfectly wrong, Doc." He grinned when he said it. "Remember that. You said I was all wrong for you."

"You are." She touched him then, the fingertips of one hand skimming along the top of his shoulder, then down his chest, across his heart. She took a much-needed breath. "Perfectly wrong, and still...perfect."

"I think you should kiss me good-morning," he said.

She frowned at him.

"Sorry." He shrugged in mock innocence and with a hint of a smile. "I've been strong and smart and careful for just about as long as I can. It's my turn to be reckless. I get to touch you now."

"Please don't," she said, both her hands coming up between them, landing squarely on his chest. She could push him away if she had to, if she had her hands between them and if she found the will.

He groaned at her soft touch, caught her by the arms and backed her up against the closed door to his bedroom, which meant no one was coming out without them knowing about it first. They were safe at the moment.

"One kiss, Samantha. Do you know how long it's been since I kissed you?"

"A long time."

"Sixty-two days," he groaned.

"Sixty-two?"

"Yes. Want to know how many hours? Because I can tell you."

"I don't know if I can leave it at just one kiss," she admitted.

"Why don't you consider it a test of will, of self-control. Let's see how much you've got."

"I've got a ton. I stayed away for sixty-two days, didn't I?"

He laughed then. Joe had the most amazing laugh. His mouth came down to hers slowly. Her heart was thundering before he ever touched his lips to hers, moving slowly and sensuously along the closed line of her mouth and then slipping inside.

An instant later he moved, his entire body in line with hers. His big hard warm body, all that skin she'd longed to touch, the thin T-shirt she wore providing hardly any barrier at all in the face of such heat. She felt every muscle in his chest and arms, felt her breasts heavy and flattened against him, clutched at his shoulders, his back, his waist.

He held her tightly, as if he couldn't get enough of her and might never let go. His tongue was inside her mouth, stroking, thrusting, and there was heat gathering low against her abdomen. She could feel it hard and straining against her, and that one kiss combusted into sheer flames in seconds.

"Joe," she protested, dizzy with it and wanting him so badly she could weep.

She wasn't the kind of woman to go up in flames in a man's arms, had never responded so freely, so recklessly to any man, and it left her head positively spinning, left her quite happy to have him holding her up when her legs turned to jelly. She simply clung to him and fought to breathe.

"Well, I guess we both flunked that little test," he said, the heat in his eyes telling her he wasn't sorry in the least.

"Joe," she protested.

"What can I do, Samantha? I see you, and I want to touch you. I touch you, and I want to kiss you. I kiss you, and I want everything,'' he said raggedly. "Everything.''

"I...I don't know what to say.''

"Can you really stay away?'' he whispered. "Can you really forget? Can you walk away from something that might be exactly what you need? What you're supposed to have in your life? Have you thought about that?''

She frowned, feeling so damned vulnerable. "It's like that for you, too?''

He nodded. "Right away. From the first time I saw you, I just liked you so damned much. It felt so good to be with you. I felt happy for the first time in a long time and hopeful and that little zing of magic. Like anything was possible, any long list of wonderful things.''

She thought she might cry. "Me, too. That's it. That's exactly it.''

"We're going to have to do something about that, Doc. We can't ignore something like that.''

"But we can't ignore everything else, either. That I'm a mess, Joe. A mess. I'm scared and mixed up and sad and hurt—all those things. And we're just the same, you and me and your kids. Have you thought about that? All of us scared and lonely and needing each other.''

"I know. You think it makes us absolutely wrong for each other, and I think it makes us right. Think about it. We know what it feels like to be hurt. We know about being careless in the choices we've made, and we want to be careful and smart now. We don't want to hurt each other.''

"No.'' He'd turned everything around, and he was confusing her terribly.

"Just think about it," he said. "Open yourself up to the possibilities. Stop looking at all the reasons to stay away and think about what we might find together. Think about how good it could be for all of us."

"I can't afford to do that."

"You won't let yourself do that," he insisted. "Just try. Tell me you'll do that much."

"Okay. I'll think about it."

"Thank you," he said.

"Will you get dressed now?" she asked, letting her eyes roam over him once more, a blush staining her cheeks.

He grinned back at her, telling her he liked having her look at him, that he knew what he was doing to her, and he liked that, too.

"I'm distracting you?" he asked.

"You know you are."

"Okay. I'll get dressed. Will you stay and have breakfast with us?"

She shouldn't. But she wanted to.

He moved closer, had her thinking he was going to kiss her again.

"Okay." She threw up her hands, stopping just short of touching him, him stopping just short of touching her. "You get dressed and I'll stay."

They were a festive group that morning. Joe made French toast. Samantha put Dani's hair in a French braid, which she loved, and even Luke, poor sad Luke, looked happy. They ate and laughed and thoroughly enjoyed themselves.

Samantha found herself still there at noon and reluctant to leave. The kids were outside playing in the backyard when she said to Joe for the third time, "I really have to go. I have to do something about my house."

"Yes, you do. You have to fire Abe. There's no excuse for the way he left that roof. He'd done a half-assed job of patching it, and things are only going to get worse the more work he does for you."

"Okay. I'll get rid of him."

"I can get the work done for you, Samantha. I'll see that it's done right. Let me do that much, at least," he said. "We won't have to see each other, if you don't want that. I'll be there during the day while you're working, and I'll be here with the kids while you're home. Think about it. How much have you seen of Abe?"

"Not much," she said.

Joe nodded. He'd made his point. She really didn't have to see that much of him, just because he was working on her house.

"Just the roof?" she asked. "And then we'll see how it goes."

"Okay."

"I...I knew I shouldn't have hired him. I did. I just...I had to move on. Can you understand that? I've spent the last year feeling so bad and just drifting along, and when I thought I wasn't going to see you again, not ever, I looked at the other parts of my life and decided I just had to do something. I had to put it back together again, and the house...it's the way I grew up, in a house a lot like this. It's the kind of place I've always wanted to live, and I thought if I could put just part of that in place in my life, maybe the rest of it would come, too, in time. Can you understand that?"

"Yeah," he said, "I do. But running away from me isn't the answer, Samantha."

"Running away could keep me safe," she said. "I step back and when my head clears and I can think, that's what I see. Running away and staying away keeps me safe."

"No, it keeps you all alone, and I don't think that's what you want or need. I just figured it out myself. I thought the same thing you did—that I just wanted to be safe, and I had to make sure the kids were safe. But that's the price for playing it safe here—being alone. I don't know if I'm willing to pay that price. Are you?"

"I don't know." She felt tears gather in her eyes. "And I can't think when I'm this close to you. When you kiss me and make me want all these things. Joe, you make me want so much."

"Me, too. I want just as much."

She sighed, thinking it only got worse. No matter what she did, things only got worse. She stepped back and said, "Thank you for taking such good care of me."

"You're welcome."

He leaned down and kissed her lightly, and the kids came and hugged and kissed her, too.

"Are you gonna come back soon for another sleep-over?" Dani asked hopefully.

Sleep-over? Samantha could just imagine how that would sound if Dani went around telling everyone she'd slept over. "I don't know, sweetie."

"And you can do my hair again? And teach Daddy to do it?"

"We do need to give your father a lesson," Samantha said, thinking that maybe they could take this slowly. Very, very slowly. Maybe if she just let herself have a little bit of him and his kids, and they were all so careful. Maybe none of them would get hurt. "What if you all come to my house next weekend? I can fix dinner for you and we'll give Daddy a lesson in French braids."

Dani beamed. So did Luke. Joe looked as if he was going to grab her and kiss her any minute.

"I have to go," she said, practically running away. This time, she was running. This time, she still had the strength.

It didn't take long for Dani's sleep-over talk to reach Joe's mother-in-law. She picked the kids up from school one afternoon a week and did homework with them and fed them dinner, a night when Joe always worked late to catch up on all he'd let go the other days when he rushed to school to get them before late-stay closed.

On Tuesday when he picked them up from his in-laws' house, Katherine Graham was waiting for him, the kids outside and out-of-the-way so they could talk privately.

"I don't mean to pry," she began.

"Dani mentioned the sleep-over?" Joe guessed.

Katherine nodded. "Really, Joe. Having a woman spend the night when the children are there? A woman you barely know? I assume you barely know her, because I can't believe you've been seeing her for any length of time. Otherwise I would have heard about it. You know how well developed the gossip system in this town is."

"I know, and it's not what you think," he said. He'd love for it to be what she thought, but it wasn't.

"Samantha just moved into an old house on Dogwood Lane. Abe Wilson was supposed to be fixing it up for her, and he left her with water coming through her ceiling last Saturday night when we had the thunderstorm come through. She came over to stay with the kids while I got a tarp over her roof, and she fell asleep before I could get back. She slept with the kids, Katherine, not me."

"Oh. I'm sorry. Dani just made it sound like—"

"I know. I've been trying to get her to stop throwing that word around—sleep-over. But she was excited. She likes Samantha, and she...she needs a mother, Katherine."

"Of course, she does. I just...I hate this, Joe. I hate what my daughter did to you all and that my granddaughter is so desperate for a woman in her life that she'd latch on to the first one that comes along."

"Samantha's a wonderful woman."

"I hope so. And I hope you'll be careful."

"We will."

"They've been through so much," Katherine said.

"I know."

"I'm sorry. You've done such a wonderful job with them, and I guess it's inevitable that you'd find someone else someday."

"Katherine, we're just getting to know each other."

"Of course, you just...you look happy for the first time in so long. Just saying her name, you look happy. And the kids seem happy, too. I thought...guess I thought it was more serious than it is."

He didn't want to think about how serious it was becoming to him already, how right it felt. She was right. He was lonely. Samantha was the first woman he'd even looked at twice since Elena left, and it wasn't that he hadn't had opportunities. He just hadn't been interested. Until now.

So was that because he was simply ready to move? Was it because he was lonely? Or was it because of who Samantha was? Because she was the right person for him and his kids?

"I like her," he said. "I really like her. But she's been through a lot herself, and we're both gun-shy."

"Good," Katherine said.

Now, if only they could stick to that plan, Joe thought.

Samantha's week dragged by so slowly she could hardly stand it. She glared at the calendar, wondering how five days could possibly last this long. They were coming on Friday evening, and she was going to make spaghetti—Luke's favorite—and chocolate cake—Dani's favorite. And she wanted everything to be perfect.

Of course, her house was a mess. Abe was furious at her and giving her a hard time about canceling their contract, and Joe's crew had been here every day, but she could tell this was going to be a long messy process. But this is what it took to put her house in order, to end up with what she wanted.

She thought about that—a long messy process. A bit scary. One where it was hard, sometimes, to see how it could possibly turn out right in the end, when things were so unsettled now, everything out of place and feeling awkward and making her uneasy. She didn't like messes. She always wanted life to be neat and tidy, everything in its place.

But life wasn't like that. Hers certainly hadn't been, and it scared her when things got so out of synch.

For the first time she thought that maybe it had to be like this now—messy and complicated and a bit scary. Maybe that was the way it worked sometimes, to get everything in place the way it should be.

Maybe she just had to learn to work through the scary times, to keep her eyes on what waited for her at the end. A place where she could feel safe and happy and secure. A place with Joe and his kids.

She wasn't thinking about the house now. She was thinking about her personal life. Maybe this was simply the way things were, the way things were meant to be.

She rushed around the kitchen Friday evening, finding bright-blue dishes and cups with clouds on them she thought Dani would think were pretty and putting out a few toys she'd brought home from her office, where she kept a supply for the kids to play with. She was ready long before they arrived, spent an entire twenty minutes sitting in the kitchen gazing out into the backyard, thinking it was ridiculous for a thirty-year-old woman to be so excited about cooking one dinner for one man and his two children.

But she was.

They came at her in a rush fifteen minutes later, the children running up the walkway and jumping into her arms. Dani gave her a sweet-little-girl kiss on the cheek and Luke squeezed her so tight. She didn't want to let him go.

"We're here!" Dani announced, sheer joy on her face.

"I know. I'm glad."

"Is your ceiling still dripping?" Dani asked, ready to go find it.

"No. Your daddy fixed it."

"Daddy fixes everything," Dani said, completely confident that he could.

Samantha stood up and watched him moving more slowly down the walkway, admiring that loose easy sway of his hips and the smile on his lips. "Yes, it seems he does."

"Does what?" Joe said, giving her a quick kiss on the mouth while the children went rushing through her house.

"She said you fix things, and I was agreeing that you seem to make everything all better."

His grin broadened. "Happy to see us, Doc?"

"Yes."

"It's been a long five days."

She nodded. "Want to know how many hours? I've been keeping track."

He laughed and pulled her into his arms. "I missed you."

"I missed you, too."

"Daddy, there's a tree house in the backyard!" Luke said, spinning to a halt five feet away and staring up at them in each other's arms. "Whatcha doin'?"

"Telling Samantha hello," Joe said, kissing her on the tip of her nose. "You said hello, didn't you?"

"Yes."

Joe's hands fell to his side and Samantha stepped back. "Luke gave me a hug and Dani gave me a kiss."

Luke frowned at that. Dani came charging into the room and announced, "There's a tree house in the backyard!"

"We know," Luke said, impatient as a big brother tended to be with a little sister.

"Can we play in it?"

"I think that's up to your father," Samantha said. "I don't know how long it's been there or if it's safe."

"We have time before dinner?" Joe asked.

"Of course."

"Okay. Let's check it out," Joe said, taking Luke and Dani with him into the backyard.

They had a great time. They ate and laughed and played, and they were so sweet. It felt so right, being with them. She found herself wishing her father was still alive, because he'd always understood magic. She wanted to ask him how he'd known when he met her mother that it was real, that it was right. What little spark of magic he'd felt that let him have no more doubts and not be so afraid. Or was she the only one who was so afraid, so cautious? So worried about taking the wrong step and it leading to disaster?

There must be some way people just know, a way to sidestep all these games and insecurities and worries.

She tested her heart, asked herself what was inside it. Pure joy at the moment. They were coming to fill up her house and to fill up her life, at least for this night.

She considered the night a complete success, and she was already asking herself when, if they were going to take this slowly, she could let herself see them again and when she could see Joe alone. She wanted to have Joe to herself, too.

It wasn't until they'd all climbed into the car and Luke ran back for the jacket he'd forgotten that she started to worry.

"You really like my daddy?" he said quite seriously.

"I like you all," Samantha said.

"But you were kissin' him an' stuff."

"Yes. Do you not want me to do that, Luke?"

"I dunno. I just..." He kicked at a stone on the sidewalk in front of her house. "Are you gonna get tired of us and go away, too?"

"Oh, Luke."

"'Cause my mommy went away. She got tired of us and went away."

"Luke, I don't know why she went away. I think that's something you should talk about with your father, and as for me and your father, and you and your sister, I don't know what's going to happen. We barely know each other."

"I know you," he insisted.

"Yes. That's not what I meant. We haven't spent that much time together. We're just friends, and—"

"Are you gonna move in with us and live with us now?"

"No," she said. "It's... Why would you think that?"

"My friend Jimmy from down the street? He's got a new daddy. His daddy left, and now he has a new one. I didn't know you could just get another one, and so I wondered. That's all."

"Sometimes when parents separate, one of them or both of them will find someone else and get married, and kids get a new mother or a new father. Sometimes both."

"If you do, you'd better not leave us," he said. "'Cause my sister was really upset. She just cried and cried and cried, and I didn't think we'd ever get her to stop."

"Just your sister?" Samantha asked gently.

"Well, Daddy wasn't really happy, either. He yelled

sometimes, and I think sometimes he cried, too, but you shouldn't tell anybody that. I don't think dads are supposed to do that, but he was really sad, and he said everybody gets sad sometimes and sometimes they cry.''

"And you?" Samantha suggested. "I bet you were kind of sad, too?"

"Maybe," he admitted.

"Luke, I don't know what to tell you. We're just not there. We're not to that point. Not nearly. We're all just getting to know each other. We all need to take some time to figure out if we like each other, and maybe, someday, if we all agree that's what we want, we could all get married and live together. But we shouldn't be worrying about things like that now. It's too soon."

"Oh. Okay." He frowned again. "But I know already. I like you. I want you to stay with us. I get a vote, don't I? Is that how it works? All of us'll vote?"

"Kind of like that," Samantha said.

"And Dani likes you, too. I know she'd vote yes, and Daddy likes you. That's three votes. That's all we need, right?"

"Oh, Luke. There's just a lot more to it than that. It's... You know how sometimes the things grown-ups do just don't make a lot of sense to you, because they're so complicated?"

"I guess so."

"Well, this is one of those things. There are all sorts of things to consider, so many that I couldn't even tell you all of them."

"You could tell me. I could understand. I'm really smart."

"Luke...I need to talk to your father about it, okay? And he needs to talk to you."

"Okay. But you like us, right?"

"I do. I promise I do."

"Then everything'll be okay."

"No. Luke!" Samantha couldn't believe this, couldn't believe how fragile this poor little boy was and what they'd done to him already, just by all of them being together a few times. She'd never imagined. Even as worried as she was, she'd never imagined it would happen this fast. "I need to talk to your father, and it can't be now because he and your sister are ready to go. They're already in the car."

"They'll come back," he said.

"No. Not now. But we'll talk. All of us will talk. But I think you should go now."

"Okay." He hesitated for a moment, then reached out and gave her a big, big hug before he turned and ran down the sidewalk.

Joe came home feeling like a million bucks, only to find a frantic-sounding message from Samantha to call him as soon as he got the kids in bed. He frowned at the answering machine as it broadcast the message. Luke and Dani were right there to hear it.

"Can we call her?" Dani asked, excited by the idea.

"No. I'll call her after I get you and your brother in bed, which needs to happen right now," Joe said. "It's late."

"But I wanna talk."

"Not now. It's past your bedtime."

Dani sulked, but he finally got her into bed. Luke was unusually cooperative, suspiciously cooperative, in fact. Which meant something was up. Joe tucked him in and said, "Have a good time tonight?"

"Yes. Did you?"

"Yes."

"And Dani did, too. Do you think Samantha did?"

"Yes. What did you say to her when you went back to get your jacket?"

Luke shrugged. "Some stuff."

Joe frowned. "What kind of stuff?"

"Just...stuff. She wants to talk to you about it."

"So she said. Anything you want to tell me?"

"Well...just that I vote yes."

"What do you mean, yes?"

"And Dani does, too. I didn't ask her, but I'm sure she'd say yes."

"Yes to what?"

"Us all living together and Samantha bein' our new mommy."

"Luke? What in the world are you talking about?"

"Jimmy Allan got a new daddy. He just moved right in, and they all got married and stuff."

"So? That's Jimmy Allan. What does that have to do with us?"

"I didn't know you could get a new one like that. I thought with Mommy gone and not coming back, that was it. But we could just find a new one, and we did. She likes us. She told me so, and we all like her. So I thought she'd come live with us, and everybody would be happy."

"Oh, Luke." Joe groaned and wanted to hit something. Himself, maybe, for not seeing how messed up his son still was by his mother walking out or by never imagining Luke concluding anything like this on the basis of nothing but seeing Samantha a few times.

How in the world could he explain this?

"It doesn't work like that, Luke."

And then his son started to cry. "That's what she said, but it could. I know it could."

"Luke!"

"You don't like her? 'Cause I thought you did."

"I do. I like her. A lot. But we barely know each other."

"But I like her, and I still miss Mommy...."

"I know. I know you do."

"And you said she's not coming back, so—"

"Luke." Joe pulled his son into his arms, and suddenly it felt as if their hearts were breaking all over again. As if it was every bit as bad as it had been when Elena left and they all just fell apart. "I'm sorry. I know it still hurts. All of it, and I'm so sorry."

"I thought everything was going to be okay. I thought we'd fixed everything 'cause we found Samantha."

"No."

"But you like her. I know you do."

"Luke, can we talk about this in the morning? Okay? 'Cause it's going to take some time for me to explain it all to you, and it's late, and we're all tired, and..." And he was falling apart. He was falling completely apart here, feeling as lost as he had when the reality of taking care of two little kids on his own hit him, feeling totally inadequate and lost and mad as hell at his ex-wife and the world in general. And feeling as if he'd failed his son once again. "I can't do this now, Luke, okay?"

"Okay," Luke said, pulling away and still crying.

Joe turned his head away and muttered a curse under his breath, thinking he'd never get this right. He'd never be able to make this all better, and what the hell was a father supposed to do except fix things like this? Protect his kids and keep anything from ever hurting them this badly?

"I can't do this now," he said. "I'm sorry. I just can't."

"Okay… Daddy?"

"Yes?"

"Did I do something wrong?"

"No, Luke. None of this is your fault."

"I made you sad."

"No. The situation makes me sad. Not you. I love you, Luke. I love you very much."

Luke held his arms open wide. "This much?"

It was a game they played. *I love you. How much? This much.*

"More than that," Joe said. "More than I can reach."

He gave his son a big hug and dried his tears, closed the bedroom door behind him and leaned his head against it and had to fight to breathe, to keep from hitting the wall and screaming in frustration or maybe sinking to the floor.

Sometimes being a parent was just too much. Sometimes he was sure he couldn't do it. That he'd never get it right or be good enough. Sometimes he thought something was wrong with the world when the person in charge decided to entrust anything as wonderful and as fragile as a child to someone like him.

Chapter Eight

It was late when he called, much later than she thought it would be. She'd had time to worry herself to death and try to find a way to tell him what she had to tell him. She had to, for all their sakes. But when he called, his voice sounded so odd, so low and tight and strained.

"It's me," he said, and that was all it took. She knew right away it was even worse than she thought, if that was even possible.

"What happened?"

"He thinks you're moving in with us," Joe said. "One dinner together, a sleep-over the night your roof leaked and a few visits to your office, and he's got us turning into one big happy family and all his troubles over and done with."

"I know. He told me!" she cried. "Joe, I'm so sorry. I never imagined."

"Neither did I."

"And I feel so foolish. I knew this was dangerous, but I was worried mostly about myself. I never imagined that Luke would put so much importance on what little bit of time we've spent together."

"I didn't, either, and I'm the one who should have realized. I'm his father."

"How is he?"

"He cried himself to sleep one more time. I swore I wasn't going to let anything upset him that badly again, but there he was, crying himself to sleep."

"Oh, no," she said, knowing she'd do the same thing. And knowing something else, too. "You know what this means. We can't see each other again."

"Don't say that, Samantha."

"What else can we do?"

"I don't know," he snapped, all his frustrations coming to bear in those three words. "And I can't think about what we're going to do right now, but don't you do this to me. To us. Don't you run away from me now."

"I'm not running. I'm thinking about your son. I don't want to do this to your son."

"I'll deal with my son. I'll find a way to explain this to him, and I'll make him understand."

"I promised myself I'd never hurt him, and I did, Joe."

"Samantha, it's the past that's upset him. It's losing his mother and how confused he still is over that, not you," he said. "We can make this work."

"I don't see how."

"We can."

"It was stupid of me to even try this. I know better. I know all about it, and I promised myself, Joe—"

"Samantha, I need to see you. To talk to you."

"It won't change anything."

"I need to see you tonight. The kids are both asleep. I can't come to you, but you can come to me. I want you to get in your car and come over here."

"Joe."

"This is too important to leave to a telephone conversation."

She closed her eyes and tried to ignore the need in his voice, the utter despair. He sounded just like Luke—heartbroken.

"It won't change anything," she insisted.

"I think it will."

"Joe—"

"Dammit, don't tell me you're the kind of woman who gives up and runs away the minute things get tough," he said. "I never believed that about you."

"I don't."

"Because I don't need another woman like that."

"I'm not."

"Then come over here and talk to me about this."

She sighed. "We really haven't started anything. It's not too late to back out. It can't be that bad to stop now."

"Is that what you really think? That you'll just close the door and never think of me again? Never miss me? Never think of what might have been between us? Because I don't believe that. I think you feel as much for me as I feel for you, and it doesn't have a damned thing to do with how long we've known each other or how much time we've spent together. I think I could fall in love with you."

"Joe—"

"That's what you want, isn't it? You want someone to love you. The way you deserve to be loved. Someone who's never going to turn his back on you and walk away. Someone who appreciates everything about you and knows how special you are. You want someone to build a life with. Someone who won't give up when things get tough.''

''I do,'' she admitted.

''I know that. I know exactly what you need, and I need you. I need you right now, tonight. I feel as bad as I ever have in my life. I nearly put my fist through the wall, I was so mad when I first came out of Luke's bedroom. I had to walk away, because I just couldn't stand it anymore. I was so mad and so frustrated, and I felt so helpless sitting there listening to him cry. And I just didn't have the words. I didn't have anything to give him to make it better.''

''Oh, Joe.''

''And then I got myself together and went back in there and sat beside him until he went to sleep, and the whole time I was thinking that there had to be a way to work this out. And I just wanted you. I needed to know that I wasn't in this alone anymore. That I could reach out for you and you'd be there. You'd listen to me and care about me and my kids and help me figure out what to do.''

''Joe—''

''That's what I need, and I honestly thought I'd have that now that I found you. I thought I'd never have to go through anything else like this all alone.''

She didn't say anything. She couldn't.

''Come to me,'' he said. ''Come now.''

In the end she went. She couldn't leave him all alone like that, because she knew exactly how he felt, and there would have been a time when she would have given anything to have someone she could call. Someone who, if she said she was feeling lost and sad and needed help, would come to her, as she went to him.

It was dark, close to midnight, as it had been the last time she'd slipped into his house. There weren't any lights on anywhere in the house, and she thought perhaps she'd waited too late, that he'd given up on her ever coming.

But as she got out of her car, his front door opened. He stood there staring at her with eyes that were dark and troubled, and when she got close enough, he took her hand and pulled her through the door. He closed it behind them and pulled her into his arms.

With a long shuddering breath, he caught her close in the dark and pushed her face to his chest and rubbed his cheek against her hair. He was trembling, she realized. So was she.

"I wasn't sure you were coming."

"Neither was I," she admitted. "But I'm not somebody who quits when things get tough, and I can't walk away now."

He took her face between his hands, and she saw the strain in *his* face, the fine lines at the corners of his eyes and his mouth, and he seemed to be hurting so badly it nearly broke her heart.

"You've done a good job with them, Joe. They're good kids, and they're probably as happy as they can be, considering what they've gone through."

"I hope so. I just didn't see this coming. I didn't see it at all."

"But you're here, and you're going to deal with it," she said. "It's just one of those things that nobody tells you how to handle. That's a lot of what parenting is—fumbling around in the dark trying your best and loving them. I know you love them, and they know it, too. I know you're patient and kind and very, very loving. The rest of it you'll figure out.''

''Thank you,'' he said. ''I needed to hear that. I need you. Here with me. Now.''

Samantha pulled his face down to hers and kissed him. He resisted for a moment, seemed caught by surprise by the kiss, but then his mouth was moving over hers, drinking from hers, savoring hers.

It was a kiss that started out as comfort and turned into something so sweet, so long and slow. It turned into everything.

He pulled back after a long moment and raised his head. ''That's not what I meant when I said I needed you here with me tonight.''

''I know. It's just…what I wanted to give you.''

It was. She wanted to give him everything, to make everything all better, to belong to him. He'd said he could fall in love with her, and she was at least half in love with him already.

She reached for him, drew him close and kissed him with every bit of longing in her soul, every bit of loneliness and fear and vulnerability lurking inside her. She wanted to absorb every bit of sadness and worry in him, every bit of despair. She wanted to take it all away.

''I need you, too,'' she said.

She wanted to pledge herself to him in the most elemental of ways. She wanted to be his, even if it was just for a moment. She wanted them with nothing between them and as close as two people could be. And it seemed he wanted the same thing. He backed her against the door and had his body, every impressive inch of his big hard body, plastered against hers in two seconds flat, while he devoured her with his mouth.

He kissed her neck and the top of her shoulder and her cheeks, her mouth once again. Her whole body throbbed with the kiss. She was one quivering mass of need and a whole pool of love. For Joe.

He lifted his head, then pressed his forehead against hers, his hot breath fanning across her lips. "We need to stop and think about this, Doc. Much as I don't want to do that. But we're moving awfully fast here—"

"Are we?" she asked, because it seemed to her right from the start that this was where they were headed. It was one of the things that scared her so badly.

"Not that I have a problem with going fast. I just want you to be sure."

"I'm sure," she said. Oh, she was.

"Sure it's what you want."

"Yes. It's what you want, too, isn't it?"

"Yes. Right from the start."

"Can we do this?" she said breathlessly. "Here? Now?"

He looked around the room, which was empty, listened to the silence. "No storms tonight," he said. "No likelihood of anyone waking up. There's a lock on the bedroom door, and I think I even have a box of condoms somewhere. A friend of mine took me out and got me drunk the day the divorce was final and told me to go forget about it all."

"Oh," she said. Of course. No one had done that for her, but—

"Hey." He took her chin and tilted her face up

toward his. "I didn't do that. It wasn't what I wanted. Sex with a stranger's never been a real turn-on for me."

"Me, neither," she said.

"I haven't been with anybody new in about a decade," he said.

"Me, neither," she said again, feeling a little giddy at the prospect. "Do you think we can manage it?"

He gave her a knowing grin. "Have a little faith, Doc, would you?"

"I do. In you."

"Come on."

He headed for his bedroom and tugged her after him. The children's bedroom doors were closed, and Joe closed and locked his bedroom door behind them. She was shivering by then, nerves and anticipation and so many things she couldn't even name.

He went into the bathroom and flicked on the light, and she followed him, not knowing what else to do. He dug through the medicine cabinet. "I know they're in here somewhere."

Samantha laughed, and she supposed she was blushing. Her lips were still tingling from his kisses, and she could feel the places on her skin where the shadowy stubble on his face had rubbed. Her cheeks felt hot and her breasts felt full and achy and her knees were shaking.

"Hey," he said triumphantly, holding up a box. "Found 'em."

She grinned at him, not remembering ever feeling this sort of joy at the idea of being with a man this way. There'd been curiosity, excitement at times, even loneliness. But not this sense of rightness, a sense that it was absolutely essential to be with him. Flat-out joy. Oh, there was joy at the thought of being with him.

He pulled her to him, then lifted her until he had her sitting on the vanity. He slid between her thighs and palmed her hips until she was nestled against him. He lifted her knees until she wound her legs around his waist, and then he took her hips again, pulling her even closer.

His mouth came down on hers once again, and she worked at the buttons on his shirt. He let go of her just long enough to shrug out of it and let it drop to the floor.

"Yours," he said against her lips. "Will you do it? I don't want to let go of you."

"Yes." She didn't want him to let go of her, either.

She pulled her shirt over her head and dropped it, too. He feasted his eyes on her for a moment and then nodded toward her bra. "That, too."

So she took that off and gasped as he settled his bare chest against hers. She felt her nipples pearl up and nestle against his chest. She opened her mouth to sigh, and he captured that, too. There was a slow wickedly sensual thrust of his tongue into her mouth and the same answering thrust of his hips against hers. She could feel him, hard and ready, with each thrust, and she wished there was nothing between them, nothing at all.

He worked his way down the side of her neck, finding that spot he'd nibbled on earlier and nearly driving her mad this time. She gasped and wound her arms around his shoulders, his head. "Joe."

"I know," he said. "I know."

It was silly to be this close to him and still want to be closer, but that was what she wanted. She couldn't hold him tightly enough, couldn't stop feeling as if he might slip right through her fingers, as if all of this might. She'd been so worried tonight, so sure it was over and done with. But it wasn't. He wouldn't let it be over, and neither would she. He was right. She couldn't forget about him and couldn't let him go.

And this was where she was meant to be. She felt it deep down inside, as certainly as she knew the sun was going to come up in the morning and set in the evening.

So she just held on more tightly and thought of truly belonging to him in every way possible, thought of creating the kind of bond that no one could ever break. Did those still exist—bonds that would never break? She wanted to believe they did, that she would have that with him.

He lifted his head from her neck and arched her back, her head falling back until it rested against the mirror behind her and his mouth nuzzling the tender skin between her breasts, the sides of them and finally the pebbled centers.

She could have spiraled out of control just at that. It had been so very long since anyone had touched her, since anyone had loved her. Honestly she didn't think anyone ever had.

"Joe," she said urgently.

"I know," he said, soothing her. "I know."

And he did. Because he lifted her with one hand, pulled at her clothes with the other, stripping off the sweatpants and her panties in one motion.

"Help me," he said, reaching for the condom.

She reached for the waistband of his jeans, unbuttoning them, pulling down the zipper and then letting her hand linger over the hardness she found there.

The next thing she knew, he'd pushed his jeans down and taken care of the condom and pulled her to him. He kissed her for a long heated moment, and she could feel him against her soft hot center. Oh, she wanted him so much she thought she might absolutely melt at any moment.

She felt his hips tense and flex against hers, felt him right at the opening of her body.

"You're ready for this?" he asked.

"Yes."

And she was. He slid inside her easily, and her whole body gripped him as tightly as her arms and her hands. None of her wanted him to go anywhere but here. He thrust easily against her, and she let her head fall to his shoulder, buried her face against his neck and took a slow shuddering breath. It rippled right through her, and he held her more tightly.

"I know," he said, and she realized he was trembling, too.

Joe, this big strong handsome sexy man was trembling for her, with need for her.

There wasn't much either of them could manage after that, except to hold on tightly and give themselves up to every bit of pleasure inside them. He kissed her and teased her and made her laugh, made her cry, and then he moved urgently against her and caught her cries with his mouth when she came apart in his arms.

She held him tightly, too, while every muscle in his body tensed and quaked and he thrust so powerfully against her and the whole world seemed to tilt on its axis.

It was beautiful and he took her to the most beautiful of places. To a place outside her body and this room and maybe even this world. To a place where there was nothing but the beat of her heart and the feel of his lips and his arms and all the love she had for him spilling over inside her and filling her entire being. Until she felt as if she could fly and that they could overcome anything that ever came between them. Until she wasn't afraid of anything and felt nothing but pure joy and happiness unlike any she'd ever known.

She cried a bit when it was over. Cried with her face buried against his shoulder once he'd carried her to his bed and slid in beside her and taken her in his arms once again.

"Oh, baby," he said. "It's all right."

"I know. It's so right," she whispered, lifting her wet face and pressing her mouth against his. "It was perfect."

"I attacked you in my bathroom, Doc. And probably rushed you and never even made it to the bed with you."

"It was perfect," she insisted.

"If you say so." He looked too serious for a moment as he wiped her tears away. "Although these scared me a bit."

"I'm just…it's overwhelming." She had to stop to breathe. "You know?"

"Yes, I know."

"It's never been like that for me," she confessed.

He drew his fingertips along her jaw, across her hot cheeks, touched the tip of her nose. "Well, I should hope not."

And then she laughed, and then he caught her close once again. They made love once more, more slowly this time, but it was every bit as powerful and as over-whelming.

A long moment later, when she was in danger of falling asleep in his arms, she said, "I have to go."

"I know. I wish you didn't have to, but—"

"I do."

"Hey, this changes everything. You know that, don't you?"

"I thought it would," she whispered. "You were right. I can't walk away. Not from you. Not the way I feel about you."

He let out a long slow breath, then gave her a gorgeous smile. He took her hands in his and brought them to his lips. "We're gonna make this work, Doc. I need you to believe that."

"I believed in all sorts of magic once."

"And you'll believe again," he said. "We'll just…we'll leave the kids out of it for now. We'll do the you-and-me part for a while. Nothing wrong with it being just you and me."

"No. Nothing at all."

"And later, when we're all ready, we'll bring the kids into it."

"Okay."

"I know I'm going to miss you tomorrow. I wish I could see you, but—"

"Luke needs you now."

"Yes."

"You'll find something to say to him, Joe. You'll find the right thing. I know you will," she said. "I know you won't let them down."

"I won't let you down, either, Samantha. I want you to understand that. From this point on, we're in this together. You and me and whatever comes along.

We'll handle it. No running away anymore. No pushing each other away. No giving up.''

"No. Not anymore."

She stayed with him for a while, curled up beside him with her head against his shoulder, just holding him, and it was wonderful to have that. Then she drove home and climbed into her empty bed and dreamed of him. Joe, who was everything good and strong and patient and kind and so very determined.

And she found herself thinking about magic—about love and hope and sheer magic. She thought of her father and mother again and how happy they'd been together. She knew how they met—on a windy late-summer day at the beach. But she wondered now what it had felt like, how he'd known she was the one.

Did he see it right away? Take one look at her and know? Was it something in his head? Or something in his heart that told him? And she tried to think of how it had been with Richard, though she thought she knew.

She met him around the time her father became ill, when she was scared and shaken and worried about losing him. Richard had reminded her of her father, although it had all been on the surface. Not appearance, but that surface image people showed to the world. She'd believed that all those qualities she loved so much in her father she'd found in Richard, and it had been sheer illusion.

Richard, in the end, had turned out to be shallow and selfish and impatient with the world, a bit childish, as well. He'd somehow gotten the idea that everything revolved around him, his happiness, his needs. And she saw now that when he was dissatisfied with his life, he assumed he could fix all that dissatisfaction by finding someone new. It was much easier than working through his own problems.

And she just hadn't seen it. She'd been in love with his daughters by then.

But she was a different woman now. An older, smarter, more careful woman. She wasn't going to make the same mistakes again. She'd found a much-different man, a simply wonderful man, and she was afraid she was already in love with him. Completely, helplessly in love. She'd probably lost her heart already to his children, too.

But that didn't mean she was headed for disaster. She had Joe now. Joe who she trusted, who had so much good inside of him.

It would all be different this time. She wasn't going to get her heart broken this time.

Joe awoke groggily from the sweetest of dreams to find sunshine, bright enough to have him wincing, coming through the blinds of his bedroom window. Dani was sitting on his chest and grinning.

"Daddy's lazybones this morning!" she announced.

Lazybones was the last one out of bed in the morning, and it was a title Joe seldom won.

"Good morning," he said, rolling her off him and genuinely happy to be alive this morning. When he had her tucked in beside him, tickling her mercilessly for a moment, he asked, "I'm the last one in bed?"

"Yes," she shrieked. "You!"

"What about Luke?"

"He's hiding! In his closet!"

"Really?" That didn't sound good.

"Yes, and he won't come out. So I came to find you."

"Well, you found me."

"Are we gonna see the fairy today?"

"No. Not today. And she has a name—Samantha."

"S'mantha," Dani said, only mangling it a bit.

"Close enough," Joe said.

"Do you think she likes us?"

"Yes," he said, wondering if Dani had gotten any ideas in her head that needed to be dealt with.

"I like her, too," she said.

"Good."

"An' I need juice."

"I think you have a cup of juice in the refrigerator waiting for you, one from last night. Why don't you get it while I find Luke?"

"Okay," she said, turning to go.

"Hey? What about me? What do I get this morning?"

She grinned again and gave him a kiss on the cheek. "I wuv you, Daddy."

"I love you, too, baby girl."

He would eat bullets for her. Leap tall buildings. Swim the widest ocean, and one grin like that one, one little peck on the cheek, made him think anything he had to do to take care of her and protect her, he would.

He had her and Luke, and now he had Samantha. He could do anything.

Joe went off to search closets until he found his son.

Luke was hiding under a blanket in his closet, with a flashlight in one hand and the jelly jar in the other. He had eight teeth. He'd lost one, and he'd gotten one from his friend Jimmy last week, but that was all. Stories were going around at school about him hurting Jenny. Everybody knew he was after baby teeth, and they were getting harder to find. All the teachers knew, too, he thought. They were watching him all the time.

He didn't know if he'd get any more teeth, except his own and maybe those of his best friend, Alex, and that just wouldn't be enough. It would never be enough.

He was trying to decide what to do when he heard footsteps outside the door, and then the closet door opened.

"Luke?" his father said.

"Yes?"

His father lifted the blanket and peered inside. "Can I come in?"

"Okay," Luke said, resigned to talking to his father.

His father climbed into the closet and sat down with his back against the side wall and got under the blanket. Luke liked it when it was just him and his father under the blanket. He pretended they were off in a cave far, far away, just the two of them.

Sometimes now, he couldn't get enough of his father. He wanted to be with him all the time.

He edged closer now, until their knees were touching, and then he leaned closer still, until he was resting against his father's side, his father's arm around him, his head on his father's shoulder.

"Better this morning?" his father asked.

"I guess."

"Luke, I'm sorry about yesterday."

"About what?" Luke thought it was all his fault. He'd gotten everything all wrong. He just hadn't understood. There was so much about grown-ups he didn't understand.

"About you being upset. I'm sorry."

Luke shrugged, then sighed, then pressed his face against his father's shirt. He was afraid he was going to cry again.

"I know you're still all mixed-up about your mother leaving, and I'm sorry. I know you don't understand why it happened and I know it feels lousy."

"Do you think she's ever coming back?"

"I don't know," his father said. "I honestly don't know. If I did, I'd tell you. I promise. But I do know that we're gonna be okay. We are doing okay, just the three of us, aren't we?"

"I guess," Luke said. It was starting to feel normal—being just the three of them.

"And whatever happens in the future, whether your mother comes back or it's just the three of us or we have someone else—someone like Samantha—whatever happens, we're going to be okay. I'll be here, and I'll always take care of you. You and I and Dani will always have each other, all right?"

"I guess so. Is Samantha mad at me?"

"No," his father said.

"You're sure?"

"Absolutely. She thinks you're great. But I don't want you to worry about her. I don't want you to worry about anything at all. You let me do the worrying, okay? I want you to think about what you want to do today. Anything at all. You and I and Dani, we'll do it."

"Really?" Luke asked.

"Anything?"

"Ice cream?" he suggested.

"Sure."

"The zoo?"

"If that's what you want."

"And we can go see the snakes?"

"Sure."

"Dani won't like it," Luke reminded him.

"I'll carry her through the reptile house and she can cover her eyes."

"She's such a baby," Luke said. "Snakes are cool."

"If you say so."

"I do." Luke felt a little better. He liked the snakes. And the monkeys. They made so much noise. He liked being with his father, and sometimes he even liked his sister, and really, it was okay with just the three of them.

"All right," his father said. "We'd better get out of here. The snakes are waiting."

Chapter Nine

He phoned Samantha that afternoon while he was sitting on a bench at the park watching Dani swinging on the swing, and Luke making a mess of himself in the sandbox.

"Hi," he said, something in him easing when he heard her voice.

"Hi. How's Luke?"

"Filthy and laughing and raising hell in the sandbox at Grant Park."

"Oh. Good. He's not upset?"

"Not at the moment. How are you?"

"I'm fine. I...I miss you."

Joe grinned. "I miss you, too, and I've been thinking about when I'm going to get to see you. I don't get a lot of time without Luke and Dani."

"Oh."

"I don't suppose I could interest you in a quick

lunch on Monday? At this messy old house I'm working on, the one on Dogwood Lane?''

"A mess, is it?" she asked.

"Afraid so. It won't be the most elegant lunch
you've ever had."

"I've always found elegance vastly overrated."

"Sounds like a woman after my own heart."

"I wouldn't mind having a little something like
your heart," she said.

She was singing in the office on Monday. Singing!
And according to her staff, she absolutely glowed. She
wasn't talking about it, but they guessed right away it
was Joe, and all she could do was blush.

"I'm taking an early lunch," she told Dixie at
twenty minutes to twelve. She'd rushed her last two
appointments and felt a bit guilty about that, but everyone was fine. Everyone's teeth were fine, and she
never played hookie from the office. She figured she
was entitled every now and then.

"Have fun," Dixie said, as if Samantha was heading off for a place like the no-tell motel.

"I'm going home for lunch," she claimed. It was
technically true.

"Nobody's as happy as you about going home for
lunch. Or are you having him for lunch?"

"Dixie!"

"Hey, if he was mine, I'd have him for breakfast,
lunch and dinner."

Samantha couldn't do anything but stand there with
her face flaming.

"Go on," Dixie urged. "Have fun."

She intended to. She rushed home, nearly drove
right through a stop sign she was so excited and dis-

tracted. Joe's truck was out front, along with three others. She hadn't thought about that—having an audience. Darn. Would she ever get the man to herself?

She headed for the front door when one of the workmen stopped her and said, "You the lady dentist?"

"Yes."

"Joe's waiting for you around back."

"Thanks," she said, heading for the backyard. He was nowhere to be found.

"Up here, Doc," he called.

She followed the sound of his voice, behind her and...up? Then spotted his face amidst the branches, in the tree house.

"Come on up," he said.

She tugged off her shoes and climbed the makeshift ladder, laughing as she went, emerging on a platform that was maybe five feet by seven perched on the branches of an oak tree. Joe took her into his arms the minute she stepped free of the ladder and kissed her soundly.

"Hi," he said.

"Hi."

"What do you think?"

She looked around, spying a picnic basket and a blanket by her feet. "Not bad."

"I didn't want to share you with the rest of them. This was the most privacy I could find on short notice," he said. "Tomorrow I thought I'd offer to buy them lunch if they all go somewhere else to eat it."

"We're going to do this tomorrow?"

"We're going to do this every day we can manage it," he said, still kissing her. "Have you ever made out in a tree house?"

"No." She laughed. "Have you?"

"No. But I'm willing to try it."

"I think I'd try anything with you," she admitted. Even risking her heart again. Even giving it away. She felt gloriously free and happy and hopeful for the first time in so long. She'd forgotten anything could feel this good, forgotten there were still things this good in the world.

"I dreamed about you last night," he said, his mouth against her ear, then nuzzling her cheek.

"I may have had a few dreams about you," she said.

"May?"

"Well..."

"You mean you weren't sure if they were about me?" His eyes narrowed theatrically, and he took a little bite of her neck.

Samantha giggled. The man made her giggle. "No, it was you."

"You're sure?" He was still tickling her neck.

"I'm sure," she said. "What am I going to do with you?"

He lifted his head and kissed her once, then again, then just looked at her. With a slow sweet smile that made her dizzy, he said, "I was thinking you should marry me."

Samantha backed up six inches and blinked, all the breath leaving her body. "Joe—"

"That's what I was thinking."

He looked faintly apologetic but dead serious. Samantha made a faint pained sound.

"And I know all the reasons why that's crazy. I know 'em all. You don't even have to say them. I still think that's what you should do."

"Y-you said we'd take it slow. This is your idea of taking it slow?"

"I said we'd take it slow in front of the kids. Not with us. You and I haven't ever taken anything slow between us."

No, she supposed they hadn't. Still... "It's only been—"

"I know," he said. "I do. And I'm perfectly willing to carry on a clandestine romance for as long as you want—as long as we think it's necessary for everybody. We can wait to tell people. For you to wear the ring on your finger. We can wait to actually take the vows. But between the two of us...I know what I want. I hope you do, too."

Samantha closed her eyes and felt the wetness of tears flooding her eyes.

"Ever been proposed to in a tree house before?" he said softly.

"No." Richard was the only one who'd ever proposed to her, and he'd done it in typical Richard fashion—in the best restaurant in town with champagne and soft music and not nearly the heartfelt emotion she sensed in Joe's proposal.

"I guess I could have waited, could have worked on my presentation a bit..."

"No." She wasn't grading him on his presentation skills but on the emotion behind the words and the utter sincerity. "You make me dizzy," she complained.

"But that's a good thing, right?"

"Dizzy," she said breathlessly. "Right now and the other night in the bathroom. It was like the whole world was spinning and I thought I might fall down any minute—"

"I won't let you fall, Doc."

"No. I know you won't. I think you're a wonderful man," she assured him.

"But I did forget one, very important part." He kissed her once again, softly, heat simmering just below the surface, need. "I'm in love with you. In a way…I didn't even know, Samantha. I've only said that twice in my life, and I didn't even know what I was talking about the first time. I'm a different man now. A better one, I hope."

"I think you're a wonderful man," she reassured him.

"But you think it's too soon."

"I think you make my head spin, and that makes it hard to think. But I miss you every second I'm away from you. And I have all these visions in my head of you and me together. You and me and Dani and Luke and babies. I'd like to have babies."

He grinned. "I know how to make babies."

Samantha started to cry then at the outrageousness of the whole situation and at how much she felt at the moment and how much she was falling in love with him.

"I'd never make Luke or Dani feel slighted in any way because someone else gave birth to them."

"I know that, Doc. I never doubted it for a minute. But you missed out on a whole lot with them, a lot of good days, days when they were so little they'd let you sit and hold them forever, just looking at them and smelling them and knowing they're absolute miracles. That two people and love can make something like that is an absolute miracle. I don't want you to miss that."

"I'd like to be there from the very beginning, at least once," she said.

"You will. You're going to make beautiful babies. We'll make beautiful ones together."

"This is crazy," she said.

"I know. Marry me."

Still, she hesitated.

"It's just you and me, remember," he said. "Just between us."

"I want to. I know I shouldn't. Not yet. But I want to."

"Then we'll do it," he said. "Whenever you're ready. You and the kids."

"I love you, Joe."

And then he kissed her, and she didn't have to think anymore.

Luke came home that day disgusted with the whole world. Danny Greene, a kid in third grade, had lost a tooth, and Luke hadn't been able to talk Danny out of it. Not for quarters or cookies or Pokémon cards. Not for anything.

He was afraid it was all over for him and his plan to collect a hundred teeth.

"Whatcha doin'?" Dani asked, as she came in and bounced onto his bed.

"Nothin'," he said.

"I got a loose tooth," she announced, sticking her finger in her mouth and appearing to wiggle one a bit.

But Luke wasn't the least bit excited. His sister was only four, and four-year-olds didn't lose teeth unless they knocked them out by accident. That was what happened to one of their neighbors. He fell out of a swing one day and when he got up, there was blood everywhere and one of his teeth was gone. They almost never found it.

Luke wasn't desperate enough to try to get teeth out of a four-year-old, and his sister had been claiming for a whole year that she was losing a tooth any day now, and it never happened.

"I'll give it to you if you're nice to me," Dani said.

"Nah," Luke said. "Forget it."

"You're gonna forget all about it? But what about the wishes?"

Luke had confided in her a few weeks ago about his plan, and now he wished he hadn't. All she did was bug him about it. Sisters were such a pain.

"I don't have enough teeth," Luke said.

"How do ya know?"

Luke thought about it for a minute. He didn't really know. He'd never known whether his plan would work. He'd just decided it was worth a shot, and a hundred was a good big number. But really, he didn't know. Samantha wouldn't talk to him about it, and he was still mad at her for that and he still believed she was the tooth fairy and that maybe she was the only one who could bring his mother back.

Of course, he'd thought for a while that Samantha would be his new mommy and that maybe they would all be happy together. That sounded okay to him, too. But his dad said he'd gotten it all wrong then, and things were so mixed up now. He still missed his mommy, and he didn't even know exactly what he wanted anymore.

"Couldn't you just try it, Luke? Try the wish, anyway?" Dani asked.

And Luke thought he might as well. He had nothing to lose except eight teeth.

That night, when his father thought he was asleep, Luke crept out of bed and got his jar of teeth. He'd thought long and hard about what to do, and he decided the first star at night was as powerful as anything he knew, and everybody said those were good for wishes, too.

He stood by his window with the teeth and gazed up at the sky, and there it was—a star. He took the teeth out of the jar and held them in his fist, closed his eyes and wished. He wished hard.

Then he put the teeth under his pillow and got back into bed.

All he could do now was wait.

"Well, I've got trouble," Joe said when he called her late that night.

It had become a habit with them over the past month. Every night she put on her pajamas and crawled into bed, and the last thing she did was have a sleepy sometimes steamy conversation with Joe.

She missed him terribly. It wasn't often they found time to sneak away together even for a conversation and even more seldom for anything else. She was still scared and surprised, hopeful and just a little bit crazy with love for him.

"What's wrong now?" she asked. Things had been settling down, she thought. The kids seemed okay. Luke hadn't gotten into any more trouble at school, and her house was looking good. Life was looking good.

"I went into Luke's room to check on him before I came to bed and stubbed my toe on a jelly jar on the floor. An empty jelly jar."

"Where he keeps his teeth?"

"Yes."

"Uh-oh," Samantha said. They hadn't had a teeth crisis in weeks. She hadn't heard a word from Luke the two brief times she'd seen him about magic or wishes.

"He put them under his pillow tonight. All eight of them. What am I supposed to do with them?" Joe asked.

"He didn't say anything about them?"

"No."

"Well…he's not after some new toy, is he? Something he'd buy if he suddenly came into a lot of cash?"

"No such luck, doc."

"Has he said anything about Elena lately?"

"Nope. I have no clue what he's up to."

"Oh, Joe."

"Maybe it just means he's done with this. This whole scheme," Joe said. "Maybe he's giving them up because he's not going to try to get any more and all of this is over."

"Maybe," Samantha said. "Or maybe he made his wish."

"Damn," Joe said. "Maybe we should offer him what he wants. A mother. You."

"Joe, it's only been a few months."

"I know. We don't have to tell them we're getting married, but we could talk about the idea of dating. We could tell him we're going steady or something. He knows about that. He watches *The Brady Bunch* on *Nick at Nite*. Marcia's going steady with somebody, and he asked me all about it. He understands going steady."

Samantha groaned. "So you're ready to turn to the

Nick at Nite School of Psychology and Child Rearing?''

"Hey, he can relate," Joe said. "And maybe he is ready to let go of this idea of wishing his mother back. Maybe he's ready to think about letting someone else into our lives. Maybe if he thought he would have someone else to mother him one day, he'd be happy."

"I hope so," she said. "What are you going to do?"

"Take the teeth and hide 'em in a jelly jar in the top of my closet," Joe said.

"You're hoarding teeth, too?"

"I thought I might. They're my kid's teeth."

She laughed again, thinking of a grown man saving each and every one of his son's baby teeth because they were as precious to him as anything else about his son.

"And the rest of it...I don't know," Joe said. "I guess we'll just have to see what Luke wants."

"You'll figure it out," she said.

"I hope so. I don't want him upset again. I want him to be happy. I want us all to move on. Together."

"We will," Samantha said.

"Soon. I want you with me. With us. All the time."

"I will be," she said.

"I'm holding you to that, Doc. Now, want to tell me what you're wearing to bed tonight?"

She laughed again. "What do you want me to wear?"

"Nothing. That would work for me."

"Sorry to disappoint you, but I'm not naked. I'm wearing my granny gown."

"The white thing. The long lacy white thing with all the buttons down the front?"

"Yes."

"Hey, I've seen that. My granny never wore anything like that to bed. I know, because when she and my grandfather came to visit, they slept in my room, and she left her nightgown lying across my pillow the whole time she was there, unless she was in it. I like your granny gown."

In truth, Samantha did, too. It was soft and kind of pretty, she thought.

"If I were there," Joe said, "I'd be working on the buttons. One by one. I'd kiss every inch of skin I uncovered—"

"Joe?"

"What? If I can't do it, I can at least think about it. Undo the buttons, Samantha. Very slowly."

"What?"

"You heard me. Undo the top button."

"Joe! I can't."

"Sure you can. You undo buttons all the time."

"Not my own." She was a bit shocked at the idea and, she admitted to herself at least, turned on just by the sound of his voice and thinking about him lying in his own bed thinking of her and all the things he'd like to be doing to her right now.

"Doc, who gets you dressed and undressed every day? Who works those buttons?"

"You know what I mean," she said.

"And I know you're shy," he said. "I bet you're blushing right now."

"What if I am?"

"I think you're sexy when you're blushing."

He should know. He made her do it often enough.

"Come on," he said. "What's a few buttons on the phone between friends?"

"You're serious? You want me to lie here and undress myself for you?"

"It won't hurt a bit," he claimed.

"Joe—"

"I miss you," he said, his voice drifting down into that deep lazy sexual tone of his that she loved.

"I miss you, too. I'll meet you for a quickie for lunch tomorrow." They'd gotten it down to a science. Clear the crew from the house. Dash into her bedroom, lock the door and he'd have her naked in ten seconds flat, and she'd find herself dying for him, her hands all over him. Every time. He'd turned her into a wanton woman, one she hardly recognized.

"Doc, I would never turn you down. Not for anything. But that's tomorrow, and I miss you tonight. Now unbutton that pretty little gown for me."

She flushed anew, heat infusing her body. She wondered if he heard that little catch in her breath, if he knew the way her breasts were tingling and had little tight peaks now. She wished he was here.

"Come on," he said. "One button. I want to see you. I want to take my time and look at you. I want to touch you. Do it for me."

"One button?" she asked.

"Just one."

She took a breath, blew it out and undid one button. "Okay. One button. Are you satisfied?"

"Far from it. Give me another one."

"Joe."

"Come on."

"It feels silly," she complained, undoing another one.

"Really? Silly? That's all you feel?"

"No," she admitted, blushing even more as she undid the second button. Her whole body was humming. It was warming and softening and opening up to him, except he wasn't here.

"Did you do it?"

"Yes," she whispered.

"Good. Give me one more," he said. "The third one's lying there right smack in the middle of those pretty breasts of yours."

"Joe," she protested.

"And they're so soft, and my hands are too rough. I always feel guilty putting my hands on them because they're so soft."

"I love your hands," she said. The skin was a bit rough in places, but his hands were so strong, so gentle. Sometimes they were so fast, so frantic. Sometimes when he was deep inside her, he'd take her hips in his big rough palms and pull her even more tightly against him. He'd pull her into that rhythm he liked so much, and sometimes when she went to pull away because the sensations were just too strong and she didn't think she could stand it any longer, he held her there against him, driving her insane. Making her into a woman she hardly recognized. One who was desperate and clinging to him and crying out his name. "Joe."

"That's it," he said. "Think about my hands. If I was there, think about what I'd be doing right now. I'd slip one hand between that pretty white gown and your skin. And you'd be so warm, so soft. I'd take one of those pretty breasts in my hand and run my thumb over your nipple."

"I know," she said. She could feel it.

"Then I'd take it into my mouth. I'd rub at it with my tongue and tease it, just the way you like."

Samantha groaned, desire throbbing through her with every heartbeat.

"Yes," he said. "Just like that. What else could I do with my mouth, Samantha? What else would you like?"

"You know," she said, letting her eyes close, letting her mind drift.

He was here, right beside her, climbing on top of her, sliding inside her, so strong, so big, stroking so smoothly. She gasped, shuddered.

"That's it," he coaxed, his voice as low and wicked as she'd ever heard it. "That's what I'd do."

He wouldn't stop. She couldn't make him. Not that she really wanted to, and he kept on, kept pushing, kept whispering to her until her eyes opened in shock and surprise. Just like that. That was all it took.

She couldn't breathe for a moment, those magical little ripplies rolling through her, that delicious warmth and that sense that all was right with the world flowing over her. She was with Joe, and everything was fine.

Except she wasn't. She was lying in her own bed alone, the buttons of her gown undone and her body spiraling down from a deliciously wicked little interlude on the phone with Joe.

Oh, it was so wicked.

"I can't believe you did that," she said.

"I didn't do anything, darlin'."

"Well, I didn't," she rushed on. "I didn't."

He laughed even more wickedly.

"You," she began, still shocked and a bit embarrassed and still so turned on she could hardly think straight.

"What? I've shocked you?"

"Yes."

"It's me, Samantha. We miss each other. I'm just trying to ease the ache a little bit."

"Well..." He had, but she didn't think she could tell him that. Not that she needed to. He knew. "I just...well..."

"What?"

"I don't do things like that."

"For me, you do," he said.

Oh, he could be so cocky at times. He could be so sexy he took her breath away, and he knew it.

"You rat!" she said, because she was a good girl. She'd always been a very good girl.

"Go to sleep and think of me," he invited. "And I'll be thinking about you. And one day soon we'll sleep in the same bed every night, and we won't have to resort to little things like this that shock you so badly, sweetheart."

"You are so bad," she said, admiringly this time.

"Go to sleep, Samantha. I'll see you tomorrow."

Chapter Ten

It was a month later that Luke caught them.

He'd rushed out the door, Dani five seconds ahead of him, to go off to spend the day with his grandparents, who'd been late picking him up, and seen Samantha arriving.

They'd played it off as casually as they could. Dani had been disappointed that she had to leave when Samantha had come over to play, and Luke had just looked at them funny and frowned.

But off they'd both gone, and the minute the door closed behind them, Joe grabbed her and pulled her into his arms. He kissed her for a long, long time, and then pulled his mouth off hers long enough to say, "Ready to go shopping?"

"For what?"

"I want you to have my ring. You can put it on a chain around your neck if you want. It can hang right there between those pretty breasts of yours all day. I'd like that, if it can't be on your finger yet.''

''Joe—''

''It's what you want, right?''

''Yes,'' she said. ''I want your ring.''

He kissed her again, long and hard. He couldn't get enough of kissing her, and he was tired of having to sneak around to do it, tired of quickies at lunch when one of them always had to rush off afterward. Tired of saying sexy things to her on the phone and shocking her and succeeding only in making him miss her more. He wanted to hold her in his arms every night in his bed. He wanted everything with her.

''And you want to marry me?'' he asked, because it felt too fragile sometimes, too fast, and he needed to hear her say it.

''Yes.''

''And live with me and my children?''

''Yes.''

''And have babies with me?''

''Yes,'' she said.

''You're gonna have a baby?''

Joe whirled around and found his son standing in the open doorway. He hadn't even heard Luke come in. *Damn.*

Samantha looked stricken and Luke looked edgy, as if he was looking at some disaster in his own living room.

''No. We're not having a baby,'' Joe said, easing himself away from Samantha and toward his son.

''That's what you said,'' Luke argued.

''No. We were talking about someday. That someday maybe the two of us would have a baby together.''

''And get married?'' he asked.

Joe stifled a groan. Luke had heard that, too?

"We've talked about that," he said as carefully as he could manage. "About someday. That maybe the two of us would be married."

"What about me and Dani?"

"You'd be with us," Joe said. "We'd all be together. We'd be a family."

"You said no," Luke argued. "I thought about that. About her being my new mommy, and you said no."

"I said it was too soon for you to be counting on that, Luke. That we were just getting to know each other, and it was too soon."

"And now it's not?"

"Now we're thinking about it," Joe said. "How would you feel about it?"

"I dunno," Luke said.

"Well, you can think about it for a while," Joe said. "Nothing's going to happen right away."

"We'd all have to want this," Samantha said. "You and Dani, too. You don't have to worry that you don't have any say in this, because you do."

"Like us voting? Just like I said?" Luke guessed.

"Yes, kind of like that," Joe agreed.

"It would take all of us to make a family," Samantha said. "If that's what we all wanted."

"I dunno," Luke said again, looking a bit uneasy and scared now.

"Well, like I said, you can think about it for a while and let us know how you feel," Joe suggested.

"Okay." Luke looked down at the floor, at his scuffed sneakers that had both laces undone and the jacket he'd dropped on the floor. "I forgot my baseball."

Joe saw it on the table in the corner. He picked it

up and tossed it easily to his son, who caught it and then stared back at them, his eyes too big for his face and his lower lip trembling.

"Come here, Luke." Joe got down on the floor and held out his arms to his son. Luke came to him and clung. "There's nothing to be scared about, okay? I told you, nothing's going to change right away. Nothing's going to happen unless we all want it."

"Okay."

"I love you," Joe said.

"I love you, too, Daddy."

"Do you want to go with your grandparents, or do you want to stay here with us today?"

Luke hesitated, obviously still thinking they were up to something and that this was indeed a very big deal. Still, Elena's parents spoiled him rotten.

"We're goin' to the ball game," he said. "Grandpa said he thinks I can catch a foul ball this time. We got seats on the end where they hit all those."

Joe nodded. "Whatever you want."

"We'll probably get ice cream. They have the best ice cream there." He turned to Samantha. "It comes in a hat. Like a baseball cap, only littler and something that ice cream won't drip through. And it's upside down, like a bowl."

"Oh," Samantha said.

"I got a bunch of 'em. I'm collectin' 'em."

She nodded. "That sounds nice, Luke."

"Do you like baseball?"

"I used to play with my cousins in their backyard when I was little."

"You did?" He looked skeptical.

"Yes."

"I bet you throw like a girl. Dani throws like a girl."

Samantha smiled and said, "I bet I can strike you out."

"Maybe we'll all play a game when your grandparents bring you and Dani home," Joe suggested.

"Okay."

And with that, Luke turned and left.

"Oh, no." Samantha said, sitting down on the sofa and looking up at Joe.

"It's all right," he said, putting his hand on her shoulder and finding that she was trembling. He leaned in closer until she rested against his side, her head pressed against him. "Luke was bound to find out sooner or later."

"Not now. Not like this."

"It's not a disaster, Samantha. Don't make it out to be. He knew months ago where we were headed. He knew as soon as I did, and I don't think this is going to cause any major trauma for him. This is his life getting back to normal and him getting what he needs, which is a mother. You're going to be a wonderful mother to him. I know that, and I think deep down, he recognized it right away, too."

"I don't know if he's ready for that," Samantha said.

"For his life to get back to normal? For someone else to love him? I think that's what he needs. I think he needs you every bit as much as I do."

"I hope so," she said. "I just…"

"You worry too much," Joe said. "Everything's going to be fine. You'll see."

It wasn't exactly fine. Not even twenty minutes later he got a frantic call from his mother-in-law, who was on her cell phone hiding out from the kids. His father-in-law was watching Luke and Dani at the moment.

''You're getting married?'' she asked, and he couldn't tell if it was shock or sadness coloring her voice.

Joe sighed and held on more tightly to Samantha, who was sitting beside him, still worrying. ''Yes, Samantha's agreed to marry me.''

''Do you think that's wise? You've only known this woman for a few months, Joe, and Elena…well…''

''You don't think she's going to come strolling through the door one day and want me and the kids back, do you? You don't think the kids and I could just forget all about the past year and half and take her back?''

''I…'' Oh, it was sadness. That was what he was hearing. ''I suppose maybe I did. I keep thinking that surely she'll come to her senses one day, that she couldn't possibly abandon her children forever, but…''

''Maybe she will one day. But I won't forget, and I don't think I'll ever be able to forgive her. I'm moving on with my life. The kids and I are moving on together. I hope you can accept that.''

''I… Oh, I want you all to be happy. I do. The kids mean the world to me, and you're a wonderful father to them. I'm so glad they have you. That through this whole thing, you've been amazing. And if you think this is wise…you and this other woman—''

''Samantha,'' he said. ''Her name is Samantha, and she's wonderful. She's kind and generous and beautiful and she's incredible with the kids.''

Katherine took a long slow breath. ''Still, it's all happened so fast.''

"Maybe. But it feels right. For both of us. Katherine, you've got to know I don't ever want my kids to go through anything again like they went through when Elena left. You have to know I'll take care not to see them hurt that way again."

"Yes. I know you will. Just…"

"It's not like we're going to run off this weekend and get married. It's nothing like that. We just decided for ourselves a few weeks ago, and we didn't plan on telling the kids so soon, but Luke walked in and caught us talking about buying an engagement ring."

"And having babies together."

"Which I sincerely hope we do. Someday. But not now. Not until Luke and Dani are both ready to accept something like that."

"All right. I'm sorry. I don't have any right to question you about your personal life."

"You're my children's grandmother. You'll always be a part of our lives. Nothing's going to change that, Katherine."

"Thank you. I needed to hear that today."

"And I think you and Tom should get to know Samantha. We're all going to be a family."

"Of course. Perhaps all four of you could come to dinner next weekend. We'll have steaks on the grill, and the kids can play in the backyard."

"Great," he agreed. "You're going to love her. Now, how's Luke? Upset?"

"More uneasy, I'd say."

"I'll take good care of him," Joe promised.

"I know."

He said goodbye and hung up the phone. He was sitting in the corner of the sofa, and Samantha was pressed against his side, her arms around him, her head against his shoulder. He leaned over and kissed her forehead.

"That wasn't so bad," he said.

"Really?"

"Yes. They're good people, and they love the kids. They'll accept this."

"I hope so. How's Luke?"

"He's okay. Just a little uneasy, Katherine said. But that's to be expected, Samantha. This is a big change in his life, and he's bound to be uneasy about it at first."

"He still wants his mother back."

"Well, he's not going to get that."

"We can't make him see it as an either/or situation. As if he has to choose—"

"There's nothing to choose between. Elena's not here."

"But I don't want to make him feel he's being disloyal to his mother by accepting me, by letting me into his life."

"You won't."

"I hope not. I want to do the right thing."

"You'll give him exactly the right thing. You'll love him, and you'll be someone he can count on. He'll realize that one day. He'll come to trust it, and he'll love you back, and everything will be fine. Believe it, Samantha."

"Okay."

"Now, can we get on with our shopping? I want my ring on your finger."

It was a beautiful ring, a lustrous milky-white pearl surrounded by diamonds, and she loved it. She let Joe put it on her finger, and she didn't take it off, although she had doubts about wearing it in front of the children and their grandparents the following Saturday when they went to dinner at the grandparents' house.

"You look beautiful," Joe said, taking her hands and pulling her to him for a quick kiss the minute she opened her door.

"Hi," Dani said, leaning around her father to see Samantha for herself.

"Hi," Samantha said, looking down at the bright shining face beaming up at her.

"Luke said you're gonna marry us," Dani said. "All of us."

"Yes, she is," Joe said, picking up his daughter and holding her between them. "What do you think of that?"

"Will you braid my hair all the time?" she asked.

"All the time," Samantha said, tears threatening suddenly.

"Daddy still can't get it 'zactly right," Dani confided, whispering in Samantha's ear.

"I'm sure he's doing his best," Samantha said. "We'll work with him on it."

Dani nodded, apparently satisfied.

Samantha looked behind them both and saw Luke, standing five feet away and looking very tentative. "Hi."

"Hi," he said, glancing at her briefly, then looking away.

She looked at Joe, who shook his head as if he didn't want her to worry about anything going on with Luke, but she worried a great deal about Luke.

"Ready to go?" Joe asked.

"Yes." She grabbed her purse, locked her front door and followed him and the kids to her car. They all couldn't fit in his truck.

They put the kids in the back, and she let Joe drive.

"Nervous?" he asked as he held open the door for her.

"Yes."

"You don't need to be. They're going to love you. Not as much as I do. No one's ever going to do that. But they'll love you."

And then she wanted to cry again, and a part of her was so scared. "Joe—"

"Everything's going to be fine," he said.

And it seemed to go just fine. Elena's parents were extremely polite, with no hesitation welcoming her into their home, and they obviously adored Luke and Dani. Still, it was awkward. How could it not be? Joe used to be married to their daughter. Still, they tried very hard, and it was going fine. Samantha kept telling herself that.

They sat on the patio and sipped iced tea, the children running through the backyard and laughing in the late-afternoon sunshine. Elena's mother seemed interested in dental care for children from low-income families and mentioned that she might be able to get one of the local charitable organizations interested in taking up the cause. Samantha did what she could, but mentioned it took a whole community of professionals, all doing their part, to make a real difference. And Elena's mother said perhaps they could work together on this, something that pleased Samantha very much. Elena's father was a retired business executive and confided that his wife could wrangle money out of the most tightfisted corporations in the state. Obviously he was very proud of her.

Dinner was fine. Very informal, served on the patio with ice cream for dessert, and Samantha was starting to relax. Although they obviously had a great deal of money, Joe's former in-laws were not pretentious at all. They made her feel right at home, and they let the children play the way children should be allowed to play. She liked them very much for that. She'd had an aunt who lived in a house like this, and going there when she was growing up was a nightmare of utterly polite and unchildlike behavior. In other words, it was no fun at all. All those breakable things to worry about, and no raised voices, no running at all. This was much, much better.

The sun was sinking fast by the time dinner was over, and Samantha found herself leaning back in a very comfortable padded chair on the patio with Joe sitting beside her sipping a beer and chatting with Tom. Dani was curled up nearly asleep in Samantha's arms. She'd come right to her, sleepy and a bit grumpy and rubbing her eyes, climbed into Samantha's lap and lay there, her body all warm and boneless. Samantha closed her eyes, savoring the sensation of having a little girl in her arms again. She couldn't quite believe how lucky she was, how her whole life had turned around so quickly and turned into something so beautiful.

She was going to have a daughter, a son and Joe, and someday babies, too. She couldn't imagine ever wanting anything more.

"Tired?" Joe whispered, leaning close to brush a hand through his daughter's hair.

"No. Just enjoying the moment."

He gave her a dazzling smile, one that could have lit up the whole town.

"I'm so happy," she whispered, as if afraid to break the magic spell that had brought her all this. It was going to take some time before she trusted it all, trusted it to last.

"Samantha," Tom said, "Luke tells us you're quite the magician."

Luke, at the mention of his name, came closer to his grandfather and said, "She pulls quarters from little boys' ears!"

"Even yours?" his grandfather asked.

"Yeah, and she let me keep it, too. And she has a bunch of fairy statues in her office and even more at her house." He looked at Samantha. "Are they gonna come live with us, too?"

Joe rolled his eyes.

"I was planning to bring all my things," Samantha said. They planned to live in her house eventually, but as Joe pointed out, there was no reason to live in a construction zone now or to rush the renovations. He had dozens of ideas about what he wanted, now that it was going to be their house, and all those special touches were going to take time. So she was moving in with the Morgans until the new house was ready.

"So they'll like…belong to all of us, right?" Luke asked. "'Cause we'll be a family, and families share."

"If you're going to share all your things with Samantha, I'm sure she'll share with you," Joe said, winking at her.

"All of 'em?" Luke asked.

"It's only fair," Joe pointed out.

"Even my Pokémon card collection? My Charizard?"

"Even that."

"I dunno," Luke said, looking highly skeptical.

Joe laughed. Samantha did, too. And soon they were all laughing. Dani stirred restlessly at the noise, and Samantha brushed her hair soothingly again.

She was thinking about itty-bitty arms curled around her, about how soft Dani's skin was, how tiny her hands were. She slipped one finger inside the open curl of Dani's fingers and felt the little girl's fingers close around her own.

It really was amazing, how little they were, how sweet they could be.

From inside the house, she heard the doorbell ring.

"I wonder who in the world that could be," Katherine said, excusing herself to answer it.

"We should go," Joe said. "Luke, let's gather up the toys you and your sister dragged out before we go."

They went off into the yard, and Tom got up to go see what was keeping his wife. A few minutes later Samantha heard some sort of commotion—raised voices. One raised voice—a woman's—and the hushed urgent tones of Katherine and Tom.

Dani stirred in her arms, and a moment later a woman burst onto the patio, a woman who looked oddly familiar. Samantha was sure she'd never seen her before, but for some reason thought she should know her.

Dani sat up, rubbing her eyes, and looked at the woman. "Who are you?"

"Who am I?" the woman said in an odd breathless way and took a step back, as if the words might have been enough to knock her to the floor.

Samantha stared at the woman again. "Are you all right?"

"No, I'm not," the woman said. "Who are you?"

"She's S'mantha, and she's gonna marry us," Dani announced, frowning and concentrating hard herself. She leaned closer to Samantha, seeming to recognize the oddly charged atmosphere of the moment and being a bit afraid of it.

Samantha was afraid, too. She closed her arms more tightly around Dani. From behind the woman, Samantha saw Tom and Katherine standing in the open doorway looking shocked and very troubled.

"Marry you?" the woman said.

"Yes," Dani whispered.

"You mean, she's going to marry your father?"

"She's gonna marry all of us," Dani insisted. "And she's gonna be my new mommy."

Oh, no. Samantha tightened her arms around Dani, who stared at the woman and asked, "Who are you?"

"I'm the old mommy," the woman said so softly Samantha doubted Dani even heard her.

Dani wasn't looking at either one of them. She was looking at her father, and the next minute she was running to him. "Daddy! Daddy!"

Joe caught his daughter and lifted her in his arms, then stood there, shock and dismay on his face.

Luke stood beside him, frozen there for an instant, and then he ran to the woman. "Mommy!"

She enveloped him in a giant hug and lifted him off the ground, too. She and Joe faced each other, each of them with a child wrapped securely in their arms, and Samantha felt sick, literally sick.

Where did she fit in this picture?

She was afraid she didn't.

* * *

She would have run right then. It was her first instinct—to run. She looked around the backyard, thinking that just a few moments ago, everything had been as perfect as it could be. She was going to marry Joe and be a mother to his lonely children. Now she worried that it would all be snatched away from her.

It wasn't the most rational thought, but there it was. What if she was going to lose everything again?

Joe was beside her. He'd come to her and put his arm around her, facing his ex-wife with her by his side and watching, grim-faced, as Luke chattered on and on, oblivious to the tension among the adults.

It was like watching an accident on the highway, Samantha decided. She didn't want to see it, but she couldn't quite look away. What in the world was going to happen?

"I should go," she said to Joe.

"No," he insisted.

"You all have a lot to talk about." She didn't even want to think about what they'd all say.

"No," he told her. "Don't go."

"I have to—"

"Samantha!"

She made a hasty apology to Katherine.

"You're goin'?" Dani asked, looking confused and worried, still hanging on to her father.

"Yes." Samantha leaned over and gave her a quick kiss. "I have to go."

"Bye, S'mantha," Dani said.

She left Luke alone. He was too caught up in his mother to notice anything else, and she didn't have anything to say to Elena. And as Samantha was leaving, she heard Dani ask tentatively, "That's her? That's my mommy?"

Oh, yes.

That was her.

"She came back?" Dani asked.

"Yes." Joe was still reeling.

Dani frowned and concentrated harder on the woman talking to Luke, who was practically dancing around her in excitement. Dani hung back, looking unsure of what to do, and Joe felt his heart breaking a little bit more, felt his anger rising and had nowhere to go with it right now. He had his kids to think about.

"Where's she been?" Dani asked. "Did she get lost?"

"I don't know, Dani."

Luke calmed down a bit, and Elena finally came over to Joe and Dani.

"Sweetheart?" she asked, a tentative smile on her face, the words oddly breathless. "Don't you recognize me?"

Dani shook her head, then buried her face against Joe's neck.

Elena put her arm on Dani's back and stroked it, pulled her hair back from her face so she could look at her again.

"How can that be?" Elena asked. "How can you not know me?"

Joe stood there, seething, wanting to tell her it had something to do with abandoning them all for a year and a half. Then he wanted to tell her to take her hands off *his* daughter. But he couldn't do that. Not in front of the kids.

"You know, it's getting late," Katherine said, stepping in and saving them. "I know Dani's sleepy, and I'm sure Luke will be soon. Why don't I take them home, Joe, and put them to bed for you?"

"Thank you," he said. "I'd appreciate it."

"I'm not tired," Luke said. "I don't want to go to bed. I want to see my mommy. She just got here."

"Yes, I just got here—"

Joe cut her off with a killing glance. Keeping his gaze pointedly on her, Joe told his son, "Your mother and I have some things to talk about, Luke. You can see her tomorrow."

And then whispering, for her ears only, he added, "Assuming she'll still be here then."

"I'll be here," Elena said, as if insulted.

God, she didn't have a clue. Even now, after all this time, it seemed she had no clue what she'd done to them.

"I don't want to go," Luke said, running to her and clinging to her.

"Tell him," Joe mouthed to her.

There was no way he was going to be the bad guy here. Let her see what she'd done to them. Let her understand a bit about their fears. Maybe if she did, she wouldn't be so careless with their feelings anymore.

Elena looked insulted and surprised and then at a total loss. Luke was clinging to her and crying. Dani was staring at her furtively when she decided to lift her head from Joe's shoulder.

"I..." Elena looked as though she might bolt for a moment, as though she couldn't believe someone wasn't going to bail her out, as they had her entire life.

"Tell him," Joe growled.

"Luke, it is late, and I do have to talk to your father. But I'll see you tomorrow. First thing. I promise."

Joe managed not to scoff at that. Her promises weren't any good here, and Luke's look told her so. God, he thought, his little boy didn't believe in too many people's promises anymore.

Katherine helped pull Luke away. Elena gave him a quick kiss, then had to disentangle herself from Luke's arms once again. He cried some more and looked at her as if he might never see her again. Elena gave Dani a kiss on her cheek and Joe handed her over to his father-in-law.

They took the kids inside, and he and Elena faced each other across the patio. She wouldn't look at him, and he let himself stare at her, every bit of anger he'd held on to over the year and a half simmering through him now.

She picked up her purse from the table by her side and fumbled around for a cigarette. Her hands shook as she lit it, he noted with a small measure of satisfaction.

He wanted to grab her by the arms and shake her—hard—and scream at her, wanted to do that so badly it scared him. He'd never hurt a woman in his life, but he wanted to now.

"You hate me," she said finally in that little girl voice he remembered so well, the one she'd used so successfully to get around any kind of anger directed at her for years. The one that made the words mean something more like, *How could anyone hate me? You don't really mean that, do you?*

God, he'd been such a fool.

"I try very hard not to even think of you," Joe said. "I don't want to waste my time hating you. I have better things to do. But yes, when I slip up and let you into my head, that's what I think. That I hate what you've done to my kids, and I can't believe I was ever so foolish to imagine you were capable of loving anyone but yourself.''

"I loved you," she said.

Joe laughed at that. "You don't know the meaning of the word."

"I did, Joe." She came to him and put a hand on his arm. He shook it off and dared her to touch him again. "I'm so sorry."

"I take it that means it's over between you and your new friend. That he wasn't really the love of your life, either."

"No," she admitted, "he wasn't. He wasn't what I thought at all."

"So he dumped you? Or you dumped him? And now you thought you'd just sail back into town and we'd pick up where we left off?"

"I wanted to see the kids," she claimed.

"Well, you've seen them. Now what?"

"I...I don't know."

"Hadn't thought any farther than that, Elena?" It was typical of her. He'd bet she was broke and thinking to come back and let her parents take care of her for a while, until she found someone else to do it or found somewhere else to go.

"I do know that what I did was wrong. So wrong," she began.

"Save it for somebody who cares, Elena. I don't."

"Joe, don't be like this—"

"Like what? Somebody who sees you for what you are?"

"I made a mistake—"

"You ran out on me and our kids. You're supposed to be the grown-up, Elena. The one they count on. The one who takes care of them."

"I did. I did it for five and a half years, and I just couldn't do it anymore."

"Oh, that's right. It was too hard. You were too unhappy. You just had to get away. Save yourself. Well, fine. It doesn't look like it quite worked out the way you expected, did it?"

"No," she whispered, "it didn't."

"Well, that's too bad. But don't think you can just come back here and say you're sorry and make everything all better."

"No, but...I'm still their mother."

"Are you? Dani doesn't even know who you are."

"I... How can that be?"

"Think about it—you've been gone a third of her life."

Elena nodded and looked at the floor. Joe still wanted to strangle her.

"But I am still their mother," she said.

"And how long do you plan on playing that role this time? Until it isn't fun anymore? Until you need to go find yourself again? Until the next rich man comes along and is willing to take you away from all this?"

"I'm not going anywhere," she insisted.

"Tell it to someone who doesn't know you the way I do, Elena."

"They *are* mine."

"They're mine," he growled.

She swallowed and backed up a step. "You mean, you're going to try to keep me away from them?"

"I mean that I'm warning you—you don't want to

cross me again. Not with these kids. If you want to see them, see them. If you want to be a part of their lives, go ahead.''

She nodded, no doubt thinking she'd won.

"But if this is some temporary whim of yours," he went on, looming over her and whispering as menacingly as he possibly could, "if you think you'll just breeze in and out of their lives from time to time over the years, with us never knowing when you'll be here and when you won't, you've got another thing coming."

"No," she said, "I won't."

"Because I will not sit here and watch you disappoint them again. So you need to do some thinking. You need to make up your mind—once and for all. You're either going to be a part of their lives or you're not. That's up to you. But don't you lie to them. Don't you lead them on. Don't get their hopes up and then disappear. Don't you dare hurt them again."

Chapter Eleven

He got out of there without killing her.

Joe considered it a victory, just to do that.

Then he stood in the driveway absolutely simmering with anger. It was rushing through him, zooming, leaving him feeling edgy and out of control and still wanting to rip somebody apart.

Elena. He wanted to rip her apart.

Why in hell did she have to come back now?

He'd spent at least six months sure that she'd come to her senses and come back, thinking it would be best for the kids and they'd muddle through somehow. He was prepared to put up with a lot for the sake of his kids. And then she'd asked for a divorce, and he'd given her one, still thinking she was bound to come to her senses. But she hadn't. And now he'd moved on.

He knew he could raise them by himself if he had

to, and he'd come to realize that what he'd felt for Elena was nothing but a boy's reckless passion, something that quickly burned out.

He'd never really known her, certainly not the way a man should know a woman with whom he had children.

Luke and Dani would be his first priority now. He wouldn't stand by and watch her destroy them again. He wasn't going to let her destroy anything.

Which made him think of Samantha and the stricken look on her face before she'd run out of here. He wanted to go to her, too, but he had to see to the children first.

He ended up having to borrow his father-in-law's car, and when he arrived at his house, Katherine was sitting on the living-room sofa with Luke curled up against her. Joe came in as quietly as possible, going to them both and seeing the remains of tears on his son's cheeks.

"He's asleep, isn't he?" Katherine asked.

"Yes." Joe bent down and picked up his son, holding him close. Closing his eyes and taking a long slow breath, Joe realized Luke felt desperately small and fragile in his arms. "He looks so big to me some days. I forget, until I hold him like this, that there's not that much to him. He's still such a little boy."

"He won't be for long," Katherine said, standing and stroking Luke's hair. "Not for long enough to suit you."

"I'm going to put him to bed."

Luke went down without stirring. He'd always fallen asleep that deeply. A fireball one minute, unconscious the next. Joe took off his son's shoes and socks, then pulled back the covers and tucked Luke in, still in the clothes he'd worn that day. Luke wasn't much for pajamas.

Joe didn't like the way Luke had run right to Elena, so excited, so eager. He was afraid for his son. And his daughter.... Joe went down the hall to Dani's room.

His daughter didn't even remember her mother. It had shocked him, although he supposed he might have expected that. Dani was so little. She hadn't seen Elena in so long. Oh, there were pictures. But how many kids had to recognize their mother from pictures alone?

He sat by Dani's bed, brushing her hair back from her face, kissing her exquisitely soft cheek. "I'm going to take care of this," he promised. "I'm going to take care of everything."

And then he went back to the living room. He thought Katherine would be standing by the door, ready to go, but she wasn't. She was still sitting on the sofa, looking as dazed and shocked as he was.

"Elena was still there when you left?" she asked.

"Yes."

"I don't want to go back there, Joe. I don't want to go back to my house, because I have no idea what to say to my own daughter."

He put a hand on Katherine's shoulder. She had been wonderful to him the whole time Elena was gone, she and her husband both.

"I bet she thought she'd just come back and say she was sorry, and everything would be okay. That we'd all be so happy to see her we'd forgive her anything," Katherine said. "And the sad truth is, we've done that so many times. So it's no wonder she'd think that. Her father and I always wanted her to have the best of everything, and we wanted to make things as easy as possible for her. Tom and I always managed to smooth out any little troubles that came her way. So I guess we taught her this—that she could do anything, and we'd take care of things for her.''

"She's a grown woman, Katherine, not a little girl anymore. She is what she is now. Her choices, her responsibility.''

"We won't make it easy for her this time. I bet she came back with no money and no job, no place to stay, and thinks her father and I will fix all that, too. But we're not going to. Not this time.''

Joe nodded. "I told her I wouldn't stop her from seeing the kids, but I'm not going to put up with her flitting in and out of their lives, either. She's got to make a decision, and I'm going to hold her to it, whatever it is.''

"Good,'' Katherine said. "It's the right thing. I'd hate it if she stayed out of their lives for good. But I know you can't let her keep putting them through more years like the one that just passed. It's too hard on them, and it's not fair to them, either. Who knows? Maybe Elena will grow up this time.''

"Maybe,'' Joe said.

"Did you talk to Samantha?''

"No. Not yet.''

"She's lovely, Joe. Inside and out.''

He nodded.

"I'm sure this has all left her uneasy. Why don't you go see her now? I can stay a while longer. I really don't want to see Elena yet.''

"Okay. Thank you.''

It was nearly eleven by the time he walked up to her door. There wasn't a single light on in the house, and that surprised him. He'd have thought she'd know he'd need to see her tonight. If Katherine hadn't volunteered to stay, he would have talked Samantha into coming to him at his house. And he couldn't quite believe she'd go home and crawl into her bed, thinking she wouldn't even be talking to him.

He was also just a little bit mad about the way she'd left him tonight.

Oh, he probably didn't have any right, and he could probably put the anger down to the fact that he'd had a lousy day, and he was mad at the whole world right now. But he hadn't liked the way it felt one bit to be standing there, so upset, so thrown by what had happened, needing her and having to watch her run away.

Deep down he realized he was blaming her for old wounds—for Elena. Which he knew wasn't fair. But then, he wasn't feeling quite rational tonight, either.

He leaned on her doorbell, hearing the sound echo through the seemingly empty house. It took two more tries and a long wait before she came to the door and stood there, wrapped in a soft yellow robe, her hair mussed, her cheeks pale, eyes red.

"Come here," he said, stepping inside and thinking to pull her into his arms.

She wouldn't, and stepped back before he got hold of her.

"Samantha?"

"Don't," she said, sounding nearly as fragile as Dani did sometimes.

"Why not?" he growled.

"Because if you touch me right now, I'm afraid I'll start to cry again, and I really don't want to do that."

"Why?" He stared at her, not understanding at all,

and the only thing he could think of that might be upsetting her was Elena's return. "You can't think that Elena coming back will have any effect on you and me."

"I'm trying to tell myself it won't," she said, turning away from him.

"Samantha!" He grabbed her then, by the arms. "Look at me."

She didn't, just stared at the floor, her hair shielding her face.

"Look at me!" he insisted, giving new meaning to the idea of being on the edge of control. *Damn.* He was shocked himself at how easy it would be to fly off the handle tonight. "You know whatever I felt for her was over a long time ago."

"Are you sure about that?"

"Yes, dammit, I'm sure. I'm in love with you."

"And what about Luke? And Dani?"

"What about them?"

"They wanted Elena back."

"Dani doesn't even know her anymore," he pointed out.

"But Luke does. He wants her."

"He *thinks* he wants her back. He wants the kind of mother he should have, not the one he got."

"Still—"

"I know he for damned sure doesn't need to be here when she walks out again, and I'm afraid that's what she'll do."

"Maybe," Samantha said. "But what if she doesn't? What if she has changed? And she wants the children back?"

"The children are mine. I got full custody in that little quickie divorce she insisted on, and she didn't fight me on that at all. She can't change her mind now.''

''She can try.''

''Let her try her damnedest. She's not going to get anywhere with that.''

''She could stay. She could have changed, and Luke wants her. She's what he's always wanted. He's going to want the two of you to get back together, too.''

''Samantha, he's a little boy. He doesn't always get what he wants. Elena taught him that, too.''

''Still, it's what he wants. You know how much he wants it, and you'd do anything for him, Joe.''

''I wouldn't get back together with Elena for anything. Not even for my son. I don't happen to think that would be the best thing for him, either. He might want it for a little while, I'll grant you that. But right now all he's thinking about is that he's so happy she's back. Pretty soon he's going to start remembering what it was like to be without her for so long, and he's going to have some hard questions for her. She won't take that well. And those excuses she's made for herself her whole life aren't going to wash with Luke.''

''Maybe. Maybe not,'' Samantha said.

''Kids know who they can count on and who they can't,'' he insisted. ''I know things are going to be sticky for a while, and complicated. Luke's going to need a lot of love and kindness and patience, and everything else we can give him. We'll get him through this, and once things settle down, we're going to get married. Please don't ever doubt that. Please don't doubt what I feel for you.''

''It happened so fast, Joe.''

"Yeah. I fell in love with you that fast. But it's real. I know it. Don't tell me you doubt all of that now."

"I do love you," she said.

"But?"

"I'm scared. I'm so scared!" she cried. "I've been here before, remember? I know what this is like."

"And I'm not Richard," he growled. He wasn't a slimy selfish bastard.

"I know."

"Do you?" he asked, getting angrier by the minute. *Damn.* "Because I really hated watching you walk away from me tonight."

"I'm sorry. I just had to get out of there."

"And if you were thinking this was going to be easy, I'm sorry, but it won't be. My life is messy and complicated right now, and maybe it always will be. I'm sorry about that, but that's just the way it is. I can't change it, and I didn't think you were the kind of woman to turn and run away when things got tough. I was betting my heart, my soul, my kids even, on that. But if I was wrong, if you are the kind to pack it in and give up, dammit, you tell me now."

"Joe—"

"Because I've been down that road. I'm not going down it again."

"I'm just scared," she whispered.

"Yeah," he said, disgusted with the entire universe tonight. "Well, so am I, and I thought…"

"What?" she asked. "What did you think?"

"That after I dealt with my ex-wife and tried to do what I could for my kids, I could come here to you and lean on you a bit. That this little crisis would be different because I wouldn't be in it all by myself—I had you. I didn't have any doubts about that. I didn't think you did, either, but I guess I was wrong about that.''

And with that, he turned and walked out the door.

''Joe,'' she called after him.

He stopped, but he didn't turn around, wouldn't even face her. ''It's not just about the good times,'' he said. ''It's not about how nice things can be when everything's going your way. Love and marriage and family is forever, good and bad.''

''I know that. It's what I want.''

''And it doesn't come with any guarantees.''

''I know.''

She put her hand on his shoulder, and he was angry enough to shake it off. He was seeing red at the moment. Anger and hurt and frustration like he'd never known. He'd been so sure this was it. That she was the one. That he'd gotten it right this time, and that he could count on her.

And he had an idea that he wasn't being quite fair to her, either, right now, but he was just too damned mad and too far gone down this road to sit back and think clearly at the moment. He'd been so sure he'd come over here and she'd take him in her arms, and he'd know that he was going to get through this with her by his side.

So fear and anger drove him on.

''You need to think about what you want,'' he said. ''Think about what you feel, what you believe deep down in your heart. Think about me and my kids and whether you're in it for the long haul, Samantha. I won't settle for less. Not this time.''

Joe awoke the next morning between two small restless bodies, Luke on one side of him, Dani on the other. She'd had a nightmare early that morning and woken both him and Luke. And Joe was miserable enough, tired enough and lonely enough that the idea of sleeping with two squirming little kids sounded good to him, so he just brought them both into his bed. They slept like sardines, but he didn't care. He wanted them close.

Dani was bouncing now. She lay facedown, her knees tucked up under her, and rocked back and forth a bit, trying to put herself back to sleep. She'd done that since she was a baby. Some kids sucked their thumbs. Dani rocked.

She used to scare him at night. She'd be in her crib, and he'd hear a thumping sound and wonder what in the world she could possibly be doing, and he'd find her rocking herself.

Luke didn't do that. He slept sideways and upside down, slept all over the bed. He was somewhere around Joe's feet right now, and you couldn't keep covers on the kid.

Joe was going to find him and drag him back up to this end of the bed, but Luke sat up first, blinked and rubbed at his eyes, and then came and lay down beside Joe.

Dani sighed heavily and snuggled in on the other side, and there they were, the Three Musketeers. He'd always told them they could do anything together, so they would get through this somehow. He would hold them all together, and he would protect them if it was the last thing he did.

"Mommy's really back?" Luke asked.

"Yes."

"It's her?" Dani asked, yawning.

"Yes, it's her."

"She looks different," Dani said.

"You don't even remember her!" Luke snapped. "You are such a baby. How can you not remember her?"

"Luke," Joe said.

"Am not," Dani said.

"Are so. You're a big baby."

"Luke!" he said more sharply than he intended. "That's enough."

Luke pouted. Dani looked as if she was working on producing a few tears for effect, to show that she was the long-suffering and most grievously injured party here. She could produce tears at will, and it had taken Joe a while to catch on to that little trick. But now that he knew, he couldn't afford to give in to her every time she did it. But God, it was hard.

"It's all right," he said, putting an arm around her and drawing her closer.

"She looks diff'rent," Dani insisted.

"I know she does. Her hair's shorter and...redder."

"I wanna be red," Dani said.

"Maybe when you're thirty, if you really want to, I'll let you color your hair," he said, kissing her cheek.

She beamed at him. "I love you, Daddy."

"I love you, too, baby." Then he turned to Luke. "How you doin' this morning?"

"I wanna see Mommy. Is she here?"

"No," Joe said.

"Where is she?"

"I bet she stayed with your grandparents."

"How come?"

"Because she doesn't live here anymore, Luke."

"But now she's back."

"Yes. Back in town."

"She's not gonna live with us?" Dani asked.

"No."

"'Cause of Samantha?" Luke asked.

"No. Because your mother and I aren't married any longer."

"You could get married again, couldn't you?" Luke asked.

"We're not going to do that."

"Because of Samantha," he said.

"Luke, even if I hadn't ever met Samantha, I still wouldn't get married to your mother again. I'm sorry, but it's not going to happen."

"So what is going to happen? Mommy can't stay here?"

"She can stay here in town, if that's what she wants. But not in this house. This is our house now."

Luke looked as if he was about to cry, and these were real tears. "You don't want her here?"

"I can't be married to her anymore. But that doesn't mean she can't be here for you. She can still be your mother."

"I don't understand!" Luke cried.

"I know." Joe hugged him close, too. "It's a hard thing for me to understand and I'm a grown-up. It must be really hard for a big boy like you to understand."

"I don't understan', either," Dani said. "An' I'm hungry."

Joe decided food should come first. Actually he thought to distract his daughter with her favorite cereal, eaten in front of the TV, even. She thought that was the ultimate treat, and there was a good chance she'd stay put so that maybe he could have this out with Luke without her hearing it all. She didn't need to hear all this. She wouldn't understand.

Once he had her settled, he found Luke in his closet holding his empty jar of teeth. Oh, no, Joe thought. He sat down in the closet with Luke and took the jar from his son's hands, thinking that maybe he knew, after all, what this was about.

"Wow," he said. "It's empty."

Luke nodded.

"All those teeth. Must have been some wish."

"Yeah. It was."

"What did you wish for, Luke?"

"That I had a mommy again." And then Luke started to sniffle. "And I think this is all my fault."

"What's your fault?"

"The mommy thing. I made the wish."

"So?" Joe asked.

"I wasn't even sure which one I wanted—my mommy back or S'mantha. I didn't even say which one I wanted, and I think now that somebody up there messed up and brought me both of 'em, and what am I supposed to do with two of 'em? You want Samantha, don't you?"

"I want to marry her," Joe said carefully. "I want her to be part of our family. I thought you did, too."

"I do. Or I did." He sniffled once again. "I like 'er, and she's kind of fun."

"But you want your mother, too?"

"Yes."

"You know, you don't have to choose between them, Luke. It's not an either/or kind of thing."

"It's not?"

"No."

"I dunno what I want, and I think I messed everything up with the teeth and the wishes. By bringin' 'em both here."

"Wishes didn't bring them here, Luke."

"You're sure? I know I never got all hundred teeth 'n' everything, but—"

"Thank goodness for that," Joe said.

"I still made the wish, and I'm sorry."

"Sorry? Why?"

"'Cause you're sad."

"I'm not—" Joe stopped right there. He couldn't lie about that. "I'm just surprised, that's all. I thought we had everything settled. I thought I knew what was going to happen. That it was going to be you and me and Dani and Samantha."

"And you like her a lot."

"Yes, I do."

"And she likes us a lot?"

"Yes, she does." Joe still believed that. He'd been rattled by the events of the night before, but he still believed Samantha loved them and that she knew how to do that. That with her, it was real and good and enduring.

"I thought we had everything figured out, too," Luke said.

"Yeah. It was nice, wasn't it? Thinking we had it all figured out?"

"Uh-huh."

"I'm afraid life's just like that sometimes, Luke. You think you understand it all, and something happens and it surprises you, and things change. But not all those changes are bad. Sometimes the changes are really good. I think this change might be good eventually. You wanted to know where your mother was. You wanted her back, and she's here now. And it's not like you can't have her in your life just because we have Samantha, too. And no matter what happens with anybody else, you'll always have me.''

Luke slipped his little hand into Joe's and leaned into him.

"Always," he said.

"Always," Luke agreed.

Chapter Twelve

Samantha eventually fell asleep, but it was very, very late before that happened. She awoke to the sound of the phone ringing from what seemed like a great distance away. But it was her phone, and squinting at the clock, she saw that she'd somehow slept until ten o'clock, which was unheard of for her.

Wincing at the morning sunlight coming through the curtains, she grabbed the phone, had it nearly to her ear before she remembered that it might be Joe, and she had no idea what she'd say to him today. She felt terrible about everything that had happened yesterday.

"Hello," she said tentatively.

"Samantha? Is that you?"

"Yes. Abbie?"

"Yes. Are you okay? You sound awful."

"So do you," Samantha said. "And it's early out there. What are you doing up at this hour?"

"I had to talk to you, and I didn't want Daddy to know."

"Oh, Abbie. We talked about this. He'll see the phone bill. He'll know."

"Well, then, he'll just have to know. I don't care if he knows. I don't even like him anymore, and I was wondering…could I come live with you?"

"Abbie—"

"You still want me, right? You said you'd always be there for me."

"Of course I still want you, and I love you very much. But we talked about this, too. He's your father."

"He doesn't like me," she sobbed.

"Oh, baby. Of course he does. He just gets frustrated sometimes, and then he gets mad, but he does love you."

"I don't think so."

"I know so." He might not be so great at showing it or at running his own life or theirs, but he did love them. "What happened now?"

"We just had another fight. A bad one. He wants us to move again. This time to California. He's got a great job offer, or so he says, and I think he and Monica are fighting. I don't even know if she's going to go, and I know I don't want to. I just wanted to come be with you, and I told him so."

Samantha sighed. Richard was always sure something better was coming along, either with people or places or jobs. Odd how she could see that so clearly now. Things got tough, he ran, just as Joe had accused her of doing last night.

First things first—she had to deal with Abbie. "Do you want me to talk to your father for you?"

"Would you?"

"Of course. I love you, remember?"

"Yes," Abbie said.

"Tell Sarah I love her, too, and I'll talk to your father today."

"Okay. Thanks, Samantha."

Samantha said goodbye and hung up. It wasn't five minutes later when the phone rang again, Richard this time. Samantha bit back a groan and wondered if the day could possibly get any worse.

"Abbie said you wanted to speak to me," he said in that smug tone she hated.

"Yes, Richard. I wanted to tell you that if you're not ready to be a father to your daughters, just send them to me. I'd be happy to have them. You wouldn't have to worry about them anymore, and they wouldn't inconvenience you in the least."

"I don't care for your sarcasm, Samantha," he said, still smug.

"I'm perfectly serious. I love them, and I'm more than willing to have them forever. I'll make whatever sacrifices are necessary—"

"You don't have any idea what it takes to raise a child, all the sacrifices involved."

"Of course I do. I'm the one who raised your daughters for three years." She had, she realized. She'd done it all and loved them. It hadn't been easy—she didn't think raising children was ever easy—but she'd loved it and found it well worth the effort. She worried that Richard didn't.

"I didn't call to listen to you criticize my parenting techniques, Samantha."

"Someone needs to, to tell you to start being a parent," she said. "You're not going to find something that's magically easier or better in California, or with some woman other than Monica or me. And you won't find two kids any sweeter or kinder or more loving than Abbie and Sarah. The problem's with you, Richard. You always think the answer to all your problems is to start over, either somewhere else or with someone else, and it's time to stop. Jeez, you're forty-five. Grow up. And if you can't, if you can't put your daughters first for a change and take care of them, send them to me. I'll see that they're fine."

"How dare you speak to me that way!"

"I dare because I love them, and it's time you started acting like you do."

"You're bitter, Samantha. Bitter because I fell in love with someone else."

"I'll never be bitter about losing you, just your daughters. Believe it or not, I'm over you, Richard. I'm in love with someone else, and I'm going to marry him."

"You're getting married?" Richard repeated.

"Yes," she said. If Joe would still have her.

Joe was right, she realized. Maybe she *had* wanted something that was easy. Something that came with a guarantee and didn't scare her at all. How ridiculous was that? And she'd panicked at the first sign of trouble. What must he think of her?

"Does this man know you're offering to take on two little girls who aren't even yours?" Richard scoffed.

"No, but he'd do it if I asked him to. He's a terrific father," she said. "You should try it. It's what your daughters deserve. Why don't you think about that for a change?''

He huffed and puffed for another ten minutes before Samantha got rid of him, and oh, she felt so much better telling him off that way. He didn't know what he had in his girls, how precious they were, the rat. And she would always miss them, always worry about them. Maybe some of what she'd said would get through to Richard. Maybe one day he'd be half the man Joe Morgan was.

Joe felt as if he'd been run down by a bus that day, knocked flat, every bone in his body aching, and he still wanted to tear something apart. Anything. And he was digging deep, looking for some patience and the right things to say to his kids.

He thought some people might say he'd been harsh this morning with Luke, laying it all on the line like that. But he didn't think he could afford to let his son build up false hope that life was magically going to go back to the way it used to be. It wasn't.

For so long they'd all thought they could just return to what they used to have, that everything would be okay, if only Elena would come back. But they couldn't. They were different now. Everything was different.

He leaned against the wall, and he was so weary he could have gone straight back to bed and slept for a day and a half. But he didn't have time for that. He had kids to take care of, probably an ex-wife to see and...Samantha.

He took a breath and held it, rubbing his forehead with his fingers.

What in the world was he going to say to Samantha?

They'd never fought about anything before. She'd never seen him the way he'd been last night. He wondered if he'd scared her by losing his temper that way, and he knew he owed her an apology.

But a part of him was in a panic, too, for the core issue remained. Did she love him enough to get through this with him? To stay and fight for their relationship?

Oh, he didn't think it had been fair of him to put it to her right then and in that way last night. But he still had to know if she was going to turn around and run when things got tough. Maybe not now, but someday in the future? What would she do when they ran into problems? Every marriage did. He was sure of that. And he felt sick just thinking about it. Losing her. Going back to the way things used to be.

She'd brought so much hope into his life. Hope and sunshine and laughter. Her tenderness, her kindness, the generous nature of her heart. All of that. He'd soaked it up like a starving man, and so had Luke and Dani.

He couldn't imagine losing her now, and he figured he had serious apologizing to do. He stopped by the florist on his way to her house when he realized he'd never even given her flowers or any kind of token of affection at all, except for the ring. He'd never really taken her out on a date, had courted her very little, and he wished it had been different, that he'd done more to show her how special she was to him.

He found something pretty at the florist, wild pink and purple flowers and soft yellow roses. He had an armful by the time he was done, and the florist merely smiled as she wrapped them up.

"In the doghouse, are you?"

"Big time," he admitted.

She handed them to him with a little wink and confided, "I'd forgive you."

Joe made it to Samantha's house by early afternoon and saw that her car was not in the driveway. He parked, walked to the front door and leaned on the doorbell, anyway. No one came to the door. He walked around to the backyard and even peered in the windows, thinking that, any minute now, someone was going to call the cops on him. But no one did.

Sighing, he looked around the backyard, up at the sky, into the trees and spied the tree house, remembering the lunchtimes they'd spent there.

And then he had an idea.

Samantha had agreed to man the dental-health booth at a health fair at one of the local malls that afternoon, and no matter how lousy she felt or how worried, she donned her fairy suit and went. She told stories and did little tricks all afternoon, passing out toothbrushes and floss and other things, and felt more than a little foolish by the time she was done.

She was remembering the first time she saw Joe and Luke, when she'd thought their problems were something she could whisk away with a swipe of her magic wand, the quarters she'd pulled from behind Luke's ear or that long swath of yellow cloth she'd pulled from Joe's pocket.

Odd, she decided as she pulled into her driveway. There were little bits of that same yellow color on her front lawn. Some pink, too. And purple.

She parked the car and got out.

They were flowers, she realized. Someone had left

a trail of flowers from her door to around the side of her house.

Her heart rate kicked up just a bit, the sadness fading by degrees.

There was a note taped to her front door, a yellow rose lying on the stoop beneath it.

She picked up the rose with a hand that shook, then the note that said, "I love you. Come and let me tell you how much. Joe."

She gathered roses as she went, around the side of the house and into the backyard, the trail leading up into the tree house.

She laughed as she started to climb, an armful of flowers and her fairy suit making it difficult. She'd forgotten all about the suit until then.

"Joe?" she called. "I want to come up, but I'm not exactly dressed for climbing."

He leaned over the narrow platform and slowly looked her over from the top of her head to the tip of her toes, and then he broke into a big grin.

"Go ahead. Laugh if you need to," she said, putting the flowers down on the ground and gathering up her skirt.

"I wouldn't dream of it," he said. "You look adorable."

"I look silly," she claimed, feeling like a little girl playing dress-up. "And if you dare make fun of me, I'll cast a spell over you."

He took her hand as she reached the top of the ladder and helped her up until she was sitting on the platform next to him, suddenly feeling shy and unsure of herself. She drew her knees up to her chest and wrapped her arms around them, her long skirt flowing around her.

He picked up a fold of the dress and ran his hand along the shiny sparkly material, and she felt even more foolish than before.

"I'm so sorry," she said.

"For what?"

"Everything."

He frowned. "Everything?"

She nodded, hoping to get through this without crying. Surely she had no more tears left. "You were right. I was looking for something easy and uncomplicated, something that offers any kind of guarantee at all that things will work out. I mean, just because it's easy and uncomplicated now doesn't mean it's going to stay that way."

"I'd say it practically guarantees it won't," Joe said.

"Yes. You're right."

"You're probably better off starting with me and the kids with everything in a mess. At least you know what you're getting into with us. Our messes are right out there for everybody to see."

"Makes sense to me," she agreed.

"We're probably doing you a favor, Doc."

She nodded. "No surprises with you."

"And we've been through so much in the past few years I figure we're due for some good times. Lots of 'em."

"I hope so," she said. "I want you all to have the best of everything."

"Well, in that case, there's just one thing we have to have."

"What's that?"

"You," he said. "Tell me we've still got you."

"Oh, Joe. I love you."

He took her mouth with his in a fiercely strong kiss, one that had her clinging to him.

"I'm so sorry," she said.

"Me, too. I had no right to jump you that way."

"No, you were right. I was running scared. First sign of trouble, and I panicked."

"I panicked a little bit myself last night, and then I took it out on you."

"No, you didn't. You were right—I should have been there for you. I should have had more faith in you. In us."

"I rushed you, Samantha. I know that. It just felt so right, right from the first moment I saw you. I don't think I'd smiled in a year and a half or so, and I know I hadn't laughed. None of us had, until we had you."

"I was so sure you thought I was a nut. A flake."

"Why?"

She glanced down at her fairy suit, and he teased the little bow on the neckline with his fingertips.

"I think you cast a spell on me, Doc. Me and both my kids. You made us remember all about magic again. Which reminds me..." He reached behind him and pulled out a jelly jar, lid on, and held it out to her.

"What is this?"

"Luke's. He gave them up for the cause, thought I might need them when I told him what I was up to," Joe said. "He even agreed to take a nap this afternoon to give the tooth fairy a chance to bring them back today, so I could see you today and not wait until tomorrow."

She took the jar and only then saw that there were a few tiny baby teeth in it.

"We only got eight," he said. "We were trying for a hundred, but it just didn't work out. But still, we thought that might be enough."

"Really?" She could hardly speak.

"There's magic in those little teeth, you know?"

"There are?"

"Yes. And wishes."

"You're making a wish?"

"Yes."

"What do you want, Joe?"

"I want you to marry me," he said. "I can't promise it's going to be easy, and I don't know what's going to happen with Elena. But then, we never really know what's going to happen in life, Samantha."

"I know that now."

"No guarantees involved, except that I love you and I need you. I need the magic and the laughter and the happiness you've brought into my life. I don't know how I could make it without you anymore, and I will do everything within my power to make you happy. I won't ever walk away."

"I know you won't."

"So." He shook that little jar of teeth making them dance around inside the glass. "What do you say? You'd be getting me. And I don't mean to brag, but I'm pretty useful to have around the house."

"Oh? Useful?" She blushed. "Good with your hands?"

"If you say so." He grinned. "I've also got two of the greatest kids in the world."

"I know."

"And eight baby teeth? Is that enough?"

"It's more than enough," she said, drawing him back to her.

"We'll make it work," he promised.

"I know, and I won't run away again, either. Promise."

Elena sat facing her worried-looking son, a sinking feeling deep in her chest that wouldn't go away. Her daughter didn't even recognize her. Her ex-husband didn't want her back at all. In fact, he was in love with someone else and supposedly getting married. Her parents had shocked her by giving her a week to be out of their house, with no offer of assistance of any kind in getting another place to live. She didn't have any money, didn't have a job. She didn't really have any skills to get a good-paying job. She'd dropped out of college to follow Joe around the rodeo before getting pregnant with Luke and getting married. And Marco, the man who'd absolutely bewitched her a year and a half ago with all the promises he'd made to her, was done with her now.

She was still shocked by how quickly that had burned out and by the way he'd just left her, as if she was nothing. It hit way too close to home, just being left like that. It was too close to what she'd done herself to Joe and the kids.

She wasn't sure she would have come back and faced the music now, except she really had no place else to go. She'd pawned the jewelry Marco had given her to live on for a while, and then when she had just enough left to get herself home, she'd run back here, a bit afraid of what she'd find and a bit ashamed, but still thinking she could salvage something of it.

She'd been so sure she could convince them all to forgive her in time. She'd always been able to do that. She smiled and batted her eyelashes. She flattered and cried a bit and begged prettily, and people had forgiven her everything.

But now Joe hated her, and her parents were ashamed of her.

Dani didn't even remember her, and now Luke wouldn't even look her in the eye.

"But why did you have to go away?" Luke asked for the third time.

So far none of her answers had been good enough, and she knew...oh, she knew there was no answer good enough. But she had missed them. As hard as her life had been here, she'd missed her kids. They could be sweet at times. There'd been times when she'd really had fun with them. But, as Joe had grown so fond of telling her, life wasn't all about fun.

And wasn't that what she'd been after when she'd run away? A little fun? Some time to enjoy herself again. It seemed as though it had been forever before she left that she'd actually enjoyed her life.

"I...I just had to get away," she told Luke.

He wasn't buying it.

"I know it was wrong," she rushed on. "And I'm sorry. I'm so sorry. I was...it was a mistake, Luke."

Again, not good enough. Joe had always been after her to grow up. Her parents had said the same thing this morning. She was almost thirty years old, she thought bitterly. She supposed it was time.

"But why?" Luke insisted.

"I just thought..." She couldn't tell him how unhappy she'd been here. She couldn't tell her little boy she'd been unhappy with him. "I don't know that I can explain it to you. Except to say that it was a mistake—a terrible mistake—and I am sorry."

But sorry didn't work anymore.

She felt panic rolling through her once again, re-membered Joe telling her it was time for her to think long and hard about what she intended to do now, to make a decision and stick to it. To be a mother or not. He wouldn't let her disappoint the kids again, and ob-viously she'd disappointed Luke badly. Her usual method of dealing with people who refused to be charmed by her, who refused to excuse any sort of mistakes she made, was to stay away from them or to run away. She didn't think she could run anymore. But how in the world could she stay?

"Are you still gonna be my mommy?" Luke asked.

Oh. She stared down at his little bewildered face. Was she?

She didn't want him to hate her, and if she kept going the way she had been, he would hate her for sure. She didn't think she could bear that. She thought about telling him that mommies were forever. Once a mommy, always a mommy, but she'd shown him that wasn't true. She couldn't do it again, wasn't sure how she'd find it within herself to stay here and face all her mistakes, all the hurt she'd caused, but...

Joe's voice came to her again from a long time ago, from one of the last fights they'd had before she left. Grow up, Elena. It's time. Think about somebody but yourself for a change.

She could do that, couldn't she? She could think about Luke and the daughter who didn't remember her.

"I am your mommy," she told Luke. "And uh...I'm going to stay here in town."

"But not with me and Daddy and Dani? That's what he said. That you weren't going to live with us anymore."

Oh, Joe had already told Luke that? "No," she said, that sinking feeling coming back again. "I won't be living there. I'll have my own place. Somewhere. And you can come visit if you like. Would you come visit me?"

Luke nodded quickly.

"Good," she said, thinking of all she had to do. "You know what, I have to find a job, too. Or maybe finish college. I never did. I met your daddy and never went back. But maybe now I will. School is…it's important."

"Daddy says so. I don't like it all that much. Just recess and lunch and seein' my friends. It's not so bad, bein' able to see your friends."

"Well, I'll remember that. I'll be sure to make lots of friends." She'd always done that easily. She wondered if she could manage it now. She again thought of all she had to do and all she owed her son. And then she remembered the woman holding her daughter the day before. "Your father tells me he's getting married again. To Samantha."

Luke nodded.

"Do you like her?" Elena asked tentatively, not sure what she wanted the answer to be.

"Yes," Luke said.

No doubts there, no hesitation. No fears. No disappointments, it seemed. Well, Elena supposed that answered that.

"Dani seems excited about having her as her new mommy."

"But you're our mommy," Luke said.

Oh. Elena had to close her eyes, hating herself more than she ever had in her life and thinking that maybe she was about to grow up just a little bit.

"You know, Luke," she began, "sometimes, people have more than one mommy. Sometimes you have one who's with you every day, one you live with, and another one you don't see as often. Maybe just on weekends or something. But they both love you, and they both help take care of you. It's just that one's there every day and one's not."

And she would not be the one who was there every day. *Oh*. She saw it then, saw it quickly in the blink of an eye. All that she'd lost. All that she'd so callously thrown away and come back too late to claim.

Luke was an amazing little boy, and she did love him, probably more than she'd ever loved anyone. But she'd failed him, and he was never going to forget the pain she'd caused him. He was probably always going to be wondering when she would disappear again.

"Do you think you could have two mommies?" she asked through a throat that was so tight every word hurt.

"I guess," Luke said. "I like Samantha. She's kinda cool. She can do magic tricks and everything. She said she could teach me how to do some of 'em."

"Really?" Elena asked, hoping she could get through this without dissolving into tears.

"Yeah, and she's got all these little fairy things. Statues and stuff. Of tooth fairies. She's a dentist, and I used to think she was magic, too."

"That's…uh…that's terrific."

"She made Daddy smile again, and she knows how to braid Dani's hair just right."

"Well." Elena cleared her throat twice before she could go on. "I was thinking that since you live with your father and he's going to marry Samantha, this could all work out, this two-mommy thing. She'll live with you and Dani and your father, and she could be your everyday mommy."

"And you'll be my someday mommy?"

"Yes." Maybe, while Joe and his new wife were giving her son what he needed, she could make something of herself and her own life. Maybe someday she could be someone her son could respect and trust again. "How would you feel? If we did it like that?"

"I guess that would be okay," Luke said, then finally looked at her again. "But you're not goin' away again?"

"No," she promised. "Not again."

Joe and Samantha were in his truck later, driving back to his house. He had his hand on her knee and was rubbing his finger in little circles, making her think of when he had his hands all over her earlier. They'd spent the afternoon in her bed, and she still felt that warm glow that came from being with him.

"Happy?" he asked.

"Yes," she said.

"I hope you're not planning on a long engagement, because I want you in my bed. Every night."

She kissed him softly, quickly. "I've never understood the appeal of long engagements."

"And the wedding? If we're not going to wait that long, we need to plan the wedding," he said.

"I was thinking we might do something really simple and small, maybe have it in my backyard."

He frowned. "Your backyard is a mess."

"But it won't be for long. I'm getting a husband who's handy, remember? And if we don't have to rush the inside of the house, because I'll be moving in with you and the kids at first, we could concentrate on the outside, just for now. The trees are budding, and everything will be blooming soon. It'll be so pretty. You and I can stand on the deck with the minister, and everybody else can be in the backyard.''

''Your deck's rotting,'' Joe reminded her. ''I suppose I should put that on my list, too.''

''You're the one who wants to get married soon.''

''Yes, ma'am,'' he said. ''We'll bring in lights and work all night if we have to.''

''You always did move fast.''

She was still laughing, still so relaxed and happy she could hardly stand it when they turned the last corner and came onto Joe's street. Samantha looked up, and she saw Elena sitting on the front porch with Luke.

''Joe,'' she said tentatively. ''Elena's here.''

He frowned.

''Did you know?''

''No.''

''And she doesn't look happy.''

''No, she doesn't.'' He gave Samantha an apologetic smile as he parked the truck, along the curb in front. ''I'm sorry. After the afternoon we had... Why don't you stay here and let me take care of this.''

''No, I want to come. If we're going to be married, she's going to be a part of my life, too, and I don't want us to be adversaries. For the kids' sake, I need to find a way to get along with her.''

Joe looked very sad for a moment, and then very grateful, as he squeezed her hand. ''I love you.''

''I love you, too. And I love your kids. Let's go fix this, whatever it is.''

He pulled the truck into the driveway, and took her hand as they walked onto the porch together. Elena stood up looking uneasy, but the chip on her shoulder that had been there the first day, the defensiveness, the anger, was gone.

"I don't think you two were actually introduced the other day," Joe said. "Samantha, this is my ex-wife. Elena, this is Dr. Samantha Carter. We're going to be married very soon."

"We are?" Luke piped up, grinning.

"Yes," Joe said. "Soon."

"Hello," Samantha said.

"Hi." Elena said nodding, hardly meeting her eyes. "I'm sorry about the other day. I was just…I was so surprised by everything."

"It's all right," Samantha said, and finally Elena looked up. She'd been crying, Samantha thought, but Luke looked okay.

Elena turned to Joe. "My mother took Dani into town for a few minutes so I could talk to Luke alone. I hope that's all right."

Joe nodded slowly, clearly having some reservations.

"And I should be going," Elena said.

"I'll walk you out," Joe said.

"And I'll take Luke inside," Samantha said.

She took him by the hand, and he came quite willingly, showing no signs of trauma from the visit by his mother. Samantha was relieved, and while she suspected there would be a lot of challenges along the way, they could deal with them. Her and Joe and the kids. It would be all right.

"I'm hungry," Luke said, heading for the kitchen and the refrigerator.

Samantha followed him as he stuck his head inside

and started rummaging around. "Find everything okay?"

"Uh-huh," he said, pushing a stool to the front of the refrigerator and opening the freezer next, emerging with a carton of ice cream and triumphantly announcing, "Double fudge, chocolate chunk, marshmallow, peanut butter swirl!"

"Oh," Samantha said, trying not to make a face at the combination.

"You like ice cream, don't you?"

"Yes."

"I love ice cream."

"But I think we should probably think about dinner first," Samantha said. "It's almost six."

Luke looked perplexed. "Ice cream could be dinner."

Samantha shook her head. "I don't think so. Are you trying to tell me your father lets you have double fudge, chocolate chunk, marshmallow ice cream for dinner?"

"You forgot the peanut butter swirl," Luke said, standing there dejectedly, still holding it in his hands. "Peanut butter's like dinner, isn't it? Sometimes we have peanut butter sandwiches for dinner."

"It isn't quite the same," Samantha said gently. "But maybe you could have a peanut butter sandwich and then ice cream."

He considered her suggestion for a moment, his brow wrinkling together, but agreed.

"It's a dentist thing," Samantha said. "We want everyone to eat good things, so they're strong and healthy."

"Oh. Okay," he said, then looked very serious indeed. "It's a mom thing, too, right? My friend Mickey

Wilson said his mom hides all the really good food in the house, and he only gets a little bit of it every week.''

''Really?''

''Yeah. It's in the back of the cabinet on the very top, but he found it and climbed up there one day to get the stuff and fell and nearly broke his arm,'' Luke confided. ''He got in lotsa trouble, and then his mom put a lock on the cabinet.''

''Oh, no.''

''Moms are really allowed to do that? Lock up all the good food?''

''I think so,'' Samantha said. ''Although I'm sure it won't come to that here. I'm sure you and I and your father could come to an agreement, and we'd all stick to the rules. We wouldn't need to hide things or lock them up. Right?''

Luke still looked troubled. ''We can still have ice cream?''

''Of course. With all the chunks and swirls you want.''

''Okay.''

''Would you like me to make you that sandwich now?''

''Okay,'' he said, putting the ice cream away. ''Does that mean you want to be my everyday mommy?''

Samantha stopped in the midst of looking through a cabinet for peanut butter. She turned to face Luke and said, ''What?''

''The everyday mommy? You know, the one who's here every day? My mom and I—'' He broke off, looking confused again. ''Am I s'pposed to still call her that? Or you?''

"We'll have to talk about it. About what you call me," Samantha said. "But Elena's still your mother. It's fine for you to call her mom."

"She's gonna be the someday mommy," he said. "But I don't guess I'd call her that. I guess I'd just call her mom."

"Someday mommy?" Samantha asked.

Luke nodded. "She told me all about it. About how some people have two, one that they see everyday and one that they only see sometimes, and she's gonna be the someday mommy."

"Oh," Samantha said, thinking that maybe Elena was going to make this easier than she expected.

"And you'll be the everyday mommy? You still wanna, right?"

"Yes," Samantha said. "I want that very much. That's what you want, too, right Luke?"

He nodded, looking terribly young and tentative in the moment.

Samantha sat down in the kitchen chair, so she could be on his level, and held out her arms to him. "I love you, Luke. And I'll be here. Every day."

He came to her and gave her the kind of hug only little people could give. The kind that came from little, bitty arms squeezing so tight. And she savored the feeling of having a little boy in her arms.

Joe came into the kitchen and stood there looking happy and touched and so very right.

"I'm going to be the everyday mommy," she told him.

"So I heard."

Luke pulled away and looked up at his father. "It's okay?"

"Sounds just right to me," Joe said, and then he pulled both of them into his arms.

Epilogue

Joe had some trouble on a construction site and didn't get home until dark. Samantha, his wife of six months, greeted him at the door, and after a warm kiss, he saw that she looked worried.

"What's wrong?"

"Luke," she said.

Joe sighed, resigned to the fact that his son was a schemer and always would be. "What's he done now?"

"He lost a tooth today."

"Oh?" They hadn't had any more tooth episodes for almost a year.

"And he's in bed already, but he wouldn't put it under his pillow. I think he's got the jelly jar again."

"You're kidding."

"No, and I'm really worried. I thought he was happy. I thought everything was okay."

"It is," Joe assured her. He'd been so sure it was.

Luke couldn't be happier with Joe and Samantha. Dani was happy. Even Elena looked remotely happy these days. She was still in town. She'd gotten an apartment with an old friend of hers from high school—a divorced woman who was starting over again, working at a temp agency during the day and going to school at night. Believe it or not, Elena was working part-time and was finishing her college degree herself.

She hadn't figured out what she was going to do with herself yet, but she seemed determined to make something of her life, and she was building a tentative relationship with Dani and had a pretty good one with Luke. He was still a little wary, but he was coming around. Elena had the kids two afternoons a week and two weekends a month, and Joe thought she was actually growing up finally, and for his kids' sake, he was happy about that.

So he didn't understand this at all.

"Nothing happened?" he asked.

"No. I talked to Elena. She was as surprised as I was."

Joe leaned down and kissed his wife. "I'll talk to him. We'll figure this out."

"Okay."

"Don't worry," he said.

"Okay."

"I love you."

She brightened at that. "I love you, too."

"Will you put on your fairy suit for me?"

She finally smiled, then laughed. "You're awful."

"No, I'm not." He kissed her one more time. "Let's go to bed early. I'm beat."

"You're beat? That's why you want to go to bed early? Because you're so tired?"

"I need my rest," he said.

"Oh? You're going to rest?"

"Well...no."

"I didn't think so," she said.

"It'll be all right. I'll talk to Luke and grab a quick shower. I expect to find you waiting for me in our bed."

He talked her into it, and he went and kissed his daughter good-night, then went into Luke's room. It was dark in there, Luke snuggled up in the far corner of the bed against the wall.

"Hey, buddy." Joe ruffled his hair.

Luke rolled over and said, "Daddy?"

"Hi. Sorry I'm late. Had a little trouble with a busted water pipe. How was your day?"

"Fine."

"Samantha told me you lost a tooth."

"Uh-huh," Luke mumbled.

"She said you might want to start collecting them again."

"Uh-huh."

"Why, Luke? I thought everything was okay. I thought you were happy."

"I am. I just need somethin'."

"Something you can't get from me?"

"I dunno. I think it takes magic," Luke whispered. "I figured maybe twenty-five teeth. That's all."

"Twenty-five, huh?" Joe puzzled over that. If a new mother took a hundred... "What do you want, Luke?"

"I want a brother," Luke confided. "People get those sometimes, after they get married. My friend

Jimmy's gettin' one, and all of us and Samantha've been married for almost as long as they have, and I just thought…well, I thought if I could get twenty-five baby teeth… Do you think that would be enough?''

Joe laughed. It bubbled out of him, a joyous sound that often echoed through their house, which he'd finished just last month. There was so much joy in their house. He couldn't believe how his entire life had been turned around so quickly.

''Luke,'' he said, ''I'll tell you what. You don't need the teeth for this one. I'll take care of it.''

''You will?''

''Yes.''

''You can do that?''

''I know just what to do,'' he assured his son.

''You're sure?''

''Hey, I found you a new mother, didn't I?''

''No, Daddy, I found her. Don't you remember? She came to my school, and I knew right away she was magic, and she is.''

''You still think so?''

''Of course,'' Luke said, no hesitation whatsoever.

''You're right,'' Joe agreed. ''She is magic. And I'm sure between the two of us we can get you what you want.''

''Thanks, Dad.''

''You're welcome, Luke. And no more teeth, right? No pulling anybody else's. No buying them out of anyone's mouth, okay?''

''Okay.''

''Good night.''

Samantha heard Joe laughing as he came down the hall to their bedroom. So it couldn't be *that* bad. She'd gotten so scared when she realized what Luke was doing, because she wanted him to be happy, and she thought he was. But Joe had taught her a lot about love and faith and strength. She loved him, had absolute faith in him, and their relationship was stronger than any she'd ever known. They could get through anything, she believed.

So this was one more little bump in the road. Whatever was wrong with Luke, they'd deal with it.

"Well?" she said as Joe came in, whistling.

"Just a second," he said. "I'm filthy, and I've got to have a shower."

"Now?"

"Yes, now."

"What about Luke?"

"I'm working on it," Joe said mysteriously.

She frowned. Joe climbed into bed with her a few minutes later. She couldn't so much as ask again what was going on with Luke before Joe had rolled over on top of her, his body hot and hard and smelling of soap.

He wrapped his arms around her and kissed her deeply, and she kissed him back.

"Aren't you forgetting something?" she said when he finally lifted his head.

"Nope, not a thing."

"Luke," she reminded him. "What's wrong with Luke?"

"I'm working on it, Doc," he said, nudging one thigh between her own and settling himself on top of her.

He started doing things to her neck that made her crazy, things that left her laughing and squirming and then just melting. She couldn't think when he did that, which was why she had to stop him now, while she still could.

"Joe," she said.

"It's all right, sweetheart. He just wants a brother, and I told him I know how to get us one of those."

Samantha's eyes lit up and happiness flowed through her. She pulled Joe closer and murmured, "Well, what are we waiting for?"

*   *   *   *   *

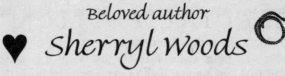

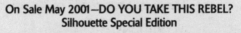

Meet 50 loving dads in

& BACHELORS USA

Take 4 FREE BOOKS,
Plus get a FREE GIFT!

Babies & Bachelors USA is a heartwarming new collection of reissued novels featuring 50 sexy heroes from every state who experience the ups and downs of fatherhood and find time for love all the same. All of the books, hand-picked by our editors, are outstanding romances by some of the world's bestselling authors, including Stella Bagwell, Kristine Rolofson, Judith Arnold and Marie Ferrarella!

**Don't delay, order today! Call customer service at
1-800-873-8635.
Or
Clip this page and mail it to The Reader Service:**

In U.S.A.
P.O. Box 9049
Buffalo, NY
14269-9049

In CANADA
P.O. Box 616
Fort Erie, Ontario
L2A 5X3

YES! Please send me four FREE BOOKS and FREE GIFT along with the next four novels on a 14-day free home preview. If I like the books and decide to keep them, I'll pay just $15.96* U.S. or $18.00* CAN., and there's no charge for shipping and handling. Otherwise, I'll keep the 4 FREE BOOKS and FREE GIFT and return the rest. If I decide to continue, I'll receive six books each month—two of which are always free—until I've received the entire collection. In other words, if I collect all 50 volumes, I will have paid for 32 and received 18 absolutely free!

267 HCK 4534
467 HCK 4535

Name (Please Print)		
Address		Apt. #
City	State/Prov.	Zip/Postal Code

* Terms and prices subject to change without notice.
   Sales Tax applicable in N.Y. Canadian residents will be charged applicable provincial taxes
   and GST. All orders are subject to approval.

DIRBAB01R   © 2000 Harlequin Enterprises Limited

Silhouette Books and
award-winning, bestselling author

LINDSAY McKENNA

are proud to present

MORGAN'S MERCENARIES:
IN THE BEGINNING...

These first stories

HEART OF THE WOLF
THE ROGUE
COMMANDO

introduce Morgan Trayhern's *Perseus Team*—
brave men and bold women who travel
the world righting wrongs, saving lives...
and resisting love to their utmost.
They get the mission done—but rarely escape
with their hearts intact!

*Don't miss these exciting stories available in April 2001—
wherever Silhouette titles are sold.*

Silhouette®
Where love comes alive™

Don't miss this exciting new Silhouette Special Edition series from Laurie Paige!

Twenty years ago, tragedy struck the Windoms. Now the truth will be revealed with the power—and passion—of true love! Meet Kate, Shannon and Megan, three cousins who vow to restore the family name.

THE
**WINDRAVEN
LEGACY**

On sale May 2001
A stranger came, looking for a place to stay— but what was he really looking for…? Find out why Kate has **SOMETHING TO TALK ABOUT.**

On sale July 2001
An accident robbed Shannon of her sight, but a neighbor refused to let her stay blind about her feelings…in **WHEN I SEE YOUR FACE.**

On sale September 2001
Megan's memories of childhood had been lost. Now she has a chance to discover the truth about love…**WHEN I DREAM OF YOU.**

Available at your favorite retail outlet.

Silhouette®
Where love comes alive™

Visit Silhouette at www.eHarlequin.com   SSEWIND